Once Upon A Whimsy

Chris Bedell

BAYNAM BOOKS PRESS

CONTENTS

1

WHAT'S IN THE TEA?

There was always something about my stepmother that I didn't understand. I would've expected her to ignore me, lock me up in the basement, or assign an endless list of chores after Father died two years ago. But no. She always smiled and treated me with respect. I'd even say she was nicer to me since Father died.

My stepmother—or Ramona, as she told me to call her—also suffered, though. Even if she didn't like being honest about her feelings. Ramona might've thought I didn't notice her behavior, but I did. Like with her rubbing her eyes, sometimes excusing herself to leave the room, or how she didn't bother getting out of bed on certain days. Just because I was only twelve years old didn't mean I was clueless.

But Ramona was the only family I had. So, I needed to at least pretend to make an effort. Like, right now, while we enjoyed our afternoon ritual of tea and cookies. Ramona didn't have to spend time with me, yet she was.

She adjusted her posture on the living room couch, then chuckled. "It used to drive my mother crazy whenever guests took their tea outside the dining room during my childhood in Whimsy."

I scrunched my eyebrows. "Pardon me?"

"My father had terrible balance," Ramona said. "So, Mother was afraid someone would spill the tea, and that he'd go flying."

I grinned at her story despite knowing better. I didn't want her thinking hardships amused me, yet Ramona's story bordered on eccentric. There were just some events that couldn't be fabricated.

"One time we were gonna go to a funeral," she continued. "And my cousin brought tea into mother's bedroom when she checked on Mother."

I beamed with my eyes, curiosity pulsing through my body. "What happened?"

"My mom was furious. Then, my cousin asked her if there was anything she could do. Mom told her to go back downstairs and have the tea at the dining room table."

I bit my lip. "Tea wasn't spilled, was it?"

"No. But the look on my mom's face was worth all the tea in Flimsy."

I remained silent. I was only several seconds away from laughing, and I couldn't have that. So, maybe, just maybe, wish fulfillment might work. If I believed I could control my amusement, then maybe I could. It was worth trying, after all. Not like my life could get any worse. That was just the reality I lived. I was an orphan—my mother died years before Father passed away.

"It's okay to laugh, Alex," Ramona said. "I chuckled when my mother shared the story."

Creepy. It was as if she had read my mind. Because I would've been lying if I didn't mention my current goosebumps on my body. Ramona might not have meant any harm, yet my thoughts should've been private.

"Don't you wanna drink your tea?" Ramona reached for a cookie, then nibbled on it.

"Sorry. Got distracted."

"No worries. That's what makes you unique."

I brought the tea up to my lips. Something acrid wafted through the air, stinging my nostrils. Not having any tea might've been rude, yet I couldn't help myself. My teachers always emphasized trusting your intuition. And I was thankful for their advice. Sometimes, a gut feeling was the only thing I had.

So, yeah. Not drinking the tea was for the best.

She narrowed her gaze, accentuating her menacing red eyes. "Something wrong?"

"The tea is still too hot, so I might wait several more minutes."

Ramona's lips curled. "No problem. Don't worry about it."

I placed the teacup back on the living room table, then grabbed a cookie. The mixture of the butter, sugar, and caramel flavors electrified my taste buds before I swallowed the cookie.

"How was your day?" I asked.

"It was fine, thanks—I did some gardening. But I used magic to put away the dishes, cups, silverware, and to straighten the house since I was exhausted."

Magic. It was an interesting word. And one would've thought magic would have solved every problem. But no. That wasn't always true—like with Father's death.

Sure. Magic made life easier. However, it wasn't a cure. People still worked. Magic just couldn't make money appear out of nowhere. The country of Flimsy wasn't a free for all. Waving my wand also wouldn't take away my grief. The grief I convinced myself wasn't there and only acknowledged by crying at night while trying to fall asleep as specs of moonlight shimmered and snuck into my room. Besides, magic was a skill like anything else. Some people were good at it, while the opposite was true for others.

She furrowed an eyebrow. "You should drink your tea, dear. It probably cooled off by now."

I grabbed my teacup. Although a vile odor once again confronted me.

Ficklewamper. I would've liked nothing more than to be wrong about the tea's unpleasant aroma. Yet I wasn't.

"I'll have the tea later." I placed the teacup on the living room table, then shoved it aside.

Her jaw twitched. "Is something wrong with the tea?"

Lying didn't matter. I had to do what was best for me. I might have not known everything, but I was smart enough to trust my intuition. The intuition that told me something was off with the tea, despite how I didn't have proof of Ramona's wrongdoing. The intuition that told me my dynamic with my stepmother might have been too pleasant. The intuition that hinted appearances weren't everything because some people hid their malicious intentions. And those thoughts only meant one thing. I had to lie.

"I'm sorry, but I'm not in the mood for tea," I said. "I'm feeling full and don't want to throw up."

She picked at her nail. "No problem."

Thank goodness Ramona hadn't chastised me for not wanting my tea. There was a good chance she tried poisoning me. And I needed a plan for dealing with Ramona. Acting impulsively because of fear would only complicate my situation.

My only problem was that realizing I needed a plan and actually concocting a solution were two different things. This was real life, not one of those bedtime stories Father read me. So, a solution might not arise as easily as it did in those fables.

"I might do some homework and then go for a walk before dinner," I said.

She scowled after looking upward. The ceiling light wouldn't stop flickering.

Ramona grabbed her wand. Then she grunted and mumbled something. A spark shot out of the wand, making the lightbulb burnout. "It was just driving me crazy," she said.

Interesting. I might not have known what Ramona was thinking. But the lightbulb incident proved she was tense. So, I wondered what thoughts currently raced through her mind. Because fully understanding Ramona was required for winning.

"No worries," I finally said.

2

BFF TIME

"You're lucky my sister isn't home," Enzo said sometime later. "If she were, then she'd complain about me socializing before doing homework,"

Enzo was both my neighbor and best friend. And we currently sat on the top step of his front steps.

My heart thumped louder and faster while sweat dripped down my back. I still hadn't revealed what happened earlier.

Enzo gave me a funny look. "Is something wrong, Alex? You aren't the stop by kind of guy."

Funny he mentioned that fact, because Enzo was right. I wasn't a spontaneous person, which meant always having formal plans when hanging out with Enzo.

I exhaled a breath. "I think my stepmother poisoned my tea."

Enzo snickered. "You've read too many books."

I nudged his shoulder. "I'm serious, Enzo."

"Why are you so certain about this?"

"It smelled funny."

"Do you think she might have added some weird spice to it?" Enzo asked.

Please. Ramona didn't add a weird spice to the tea. She made it the same way every day—up until today—which entailed only honey and three sugar packets.

But no. I wouldn't argue with Enzo. Alienating him would only make life more complicated, and that was the last thing I needed when trying to figure out what I'd do about Ramona.

"Nope," I said.

Enzo's eyes narrowed. "Can you think of anything you did to make her angry?"

I shrugged. "Nope."

He gritted his teeth. "I'm sorry, but I don't know what to say..."

"Listening helps."

Enzo patted my knee. "You know I'd do anything for you."

"As would I."

He coughed into his right arm. "If she really tried to kill you, then you need a plan."

I hung my head lower. "I know, I know."

Tree branches rustled after the whistling wind grew louder, pushing a piece of paper towards me.

I picked up the poster, then scanned it. I had seen the paper plastered on every tree and mailbox in the thirty something square miles that was Flimsy.

The poster I picked up was a HELP WANTED call from Marino the Great. He was one of the most powerful people in Flimsy. He was a magician, who spent years studying magic. Everyone in Flimsy was born with magic, yet some people were still impressed with Marino the Great putting on magic shows. Not everyone was skilled with magic like him. Father even once referred to Marino the Great as a "lazy bum." He thought Marino the Great needed a more serious career.

Marino the Great wasn't immortal, though. He caught a curse and was going to die within a year. He wanted someone to fetch a crystal from the Kuku mountains in the neighboring country of Whimsy. The crystal would grant him a wish, which was to see his dead wife one last time. Marino was unable to make the voyage himself, because the curse made him too weak to travel such a great distance. So, in return, he promised to give the person anything he or she wanted. Yet I didn't think anyone had accepted his offer yet. The posters remained plastered everywhere. So, maybe, just maybe, I could get help with Ramona if I visited Marino the Great's shop in town.

"What is it?" Enzo asked.

"I know what to do."

His eyes drifted to the poster. "Don't tell me you're serious?"

"It's the only option I have."

He rolled his eyes. "Whatever."

I gave Enzo a dirty look. Being my best friend meant Enzo should've supported me unconditionally. Especially when Ramona just tried to kill me.

"Sorry," Enzo continued. "I shouldn't have been so blunt."

"Thank you." I stood.

"Don't tell Hanna I'm outside instead of doing homework if you see her."

"What makes you think I'll run into her?"

"She went to the store to buy groceries."

Yup. Enzo hadn't misspoken by saying his sister bought groceries instead of his parents. Hanna was Enzo's guardian. But Enzo's home life was a story for another day. Contemplating Enzo's hard life was the last thing I needed to do. Not when dealing with Ramona was my most urgent problem.

I chuckled. "Okay."

Enzo smirked. "Good luck."

"Thanks. I'll need it."

I descended Enzo's front steps without another word.

Wind swooshed through the air while relief washed over me. Even just chatting with Enzo was enough to calm me, proving our teachers were right. Secrets often made problems worse. Dealing with an issue was bad enough, but not having a friend to confide in often complicated life. Nobody deserved to go through life alone. And as long as Enzo was in my life, then I'd be fine.

3

WE HAVE A DEAL

The placard clanked against the door after I entered Marino the Great's shop half an hour later.

My pulse hammered in my ears while I caught my breath. The shop wasn't far away, but I scurried to the shop as if a crocodile chomped at my heels. Speed was my only option. The sooner I dealt with Ramona, the sooner my life would return to normal.

I scratched my chin. Marino the Great wasn't by the cash register.

My gaze shifted to the bell in front of the cash register, and I rang it twice.

The break room door behind the counter opened, revealing a cloaked figure. The person closed the remaining distance between the door and the glass display before standing in front of me.

The person lifted his hood, revealing his sallow skin and stringy hair, which was more grey than black.

The guy standing in front of me was definitely Marino the Great. I had seen his face numerous times before. It was on the posters he hung up everywhere, besides how I learned about him in school in one of my history classes.

Marino sighed. "Sorry. Just finishing a late lunch."

"Don't worry about it," I said.

"How can I help you?" he asked.

"Is your offer still good?"

He nodded. "Yes. But why do you ask?"

"I wanna accept it."

"You're only a kid."

In a perfect world, Marino the Great wouldn't have criticized my age, yet life was anything but perfect. So, I'd take a few deep breaths while thinking about something that made me happy. Like Enzo or cookies. Both things were important to my life.

"I need help defeating my stepmother," I revealed.

He snorted. "Why?"

I exhaled a long breath. "She tried to poison me."

His jaw lowered. "Oh..."

"So, I'm gonna need your help."

"Well, you're the only volunteer," Marino stammered.

My eyes widened. "Do we have a deal?"

"Yes." He offered his hand.

"Great," I said, shaking his hand.

Ficklewamper. Marino might have been dying from a curse. But he gave a firm handshake, because my hand would have broken if he gripped it any harder.

"Anyway, I'll give you a couple of things to help you." Marino the Great searched the space behind him.

I remained silent while Marino the Great fetched the items.

For a split-second, I couldn't help wondering what life would be like if I owned this shop. Having a business would've meant interacting with people. Yet something exciting existed from dealing with the public. I'd never know what to expect when a new customer entered the shop. And that fact fascinated me. A little mystery was what made life worth living. Life would've been boring if it was always predictable.

"This is a map with the x on the Kuku Mountains where the crystal is located, and here's a necklace. Three taps, and you'll be able to communicate with me in an emergency," he said after handing the things to me.

I squinted at the map, then a realization hit me. "The Kuku mountains are on the other side of Whimsy."

"Will that be a problem?" Marino asked.

I didn't even stutter. "No, everything is fine."

Marino rubbed his hands together, glee beaming from his eyes. "Good."

"How do I know the necklace will work in Whimsy?"

"It will."

No offense, but I needed more than his word. I had enough anxiety without having to explain my absence to Ramona, and I didn't need the increased pressure of wondering if my trip would be successful.

His eyebrows knitted together. "Something wrong?"

"That obvious?"

He chuckled. "I'm good at reading people."

"I don't want anything to go wrong."

Marino the Great exhaled a deep breath. "Look at it this way. You're doing what you've gotta do to defeat your stepmother."

When he was right, he was right. I couldn't fault Marino the Great for what he said. Trying to poison me was a concrete fact, and Ramona needed to be dealt with. Besides, if I wasn't journeying to Whimsy, then it'd just be something else giving me anxiety.

4

OFF TO WHIMSY

I almost opened the front door and left my home after packing clothing and snacks when someone cackled.

That voice. I would've recognized the hoarse tone anywhere. It was Ramona.

My throat tightened. I would've given anything to flee my home without Ramona noticing me. Yet life had other plans, and I needed to hope I'd survive this interaction with Ramona. The only thing worse than false hope was no hope.

Ramona continued standing by the kitchen's entrance. "I was worried about you, Alex. You didn't say anything when you returned from your walk and just went straight to your bedroom."

"I didn't wanna bother you."

"You're never a bother." Ramona's gaze shifted to my sac. "Going somewhere?"

"I was gonna camp in Enzo's backyard tonight," I revealed. "Is that okay?"

Ramona sucked in a breath. "Sure. But I feel bad you didn't have your afternoon tea."

"I was full."

"Yeah, that's what you said." Ramona paused for a beat, eyes remaining glued to me. "But you almost seemed afraid of your tea. Was there something wrong with your tea?"

"I don't know. You tell me."

Caring about seeming fresh was irrelevant—not when my life was at stake. I could always apologize to Ramona if I was wrong about her poisoning me.

"Excuse me?" Ramona asked.

I grunted. "It was more than something being wrong with my tea. It was poisoned."

Ramona clutched her pearl necklace. "I don't know why you'd say that."

"I might be a lot of things, but I'm not stupid.

"Ficklewamper." Ramona jabbed her fists. "I knew I should've gone with a more expensive poison."

Thump. Thump. Thump. There it was again. My increased heartbeat. Because I had every reason for the anger bubbling inside me. Ramona actually said the word, "poison." So, the issue of her poisoning me was no longer a hypothetical situation.

Ramona shook her head. "I should've put more effort into my plan. It's just so wrong that Richard left you the rubies."

No. Ramona didn't misspeak, no matter how odd it might've seemed for a twelve-year-old to inherit something. Twelve was the age of majority. Okay. Fine. More like supervised majority. People still lived at home till eighteen while spending six years as an apprentice in a chosen career field.

"That's what it's about? You said you weren't mad?" I asked.

She shrieked. "I lied."

"You really wanted to poison me?" I stammered.

She nodded. "And it would've worked. Poisoning you would've mimicked the symptoms of the Flail, and nobody would have suspected a thing."

"The last two years were a lie?"

"You didn't think I enjoyed being your stepmother, did you?" Ramona asked. "Because the law dictates that I can only get the rubies if you die, since I'm your only family."

"Wow. And people think I'm eccentric." I put my hand behind me, grabbing my wand. I kept it there while I stared at her.

She cackled. "I'll just use magic to kill you. Although I had to wait two blasted years to kill you. Dying so close to Richard's death would've made people suspicious."

"You hate me that much?" I asked.

"Haven't you been paying attention? This isn't about you. It's about building a better life for myself. Let's just say the rubies aren't my first disappointment."

"What do you mean?"

"Duh," Ramona said. "I hate my sister because she took everything from me years ago."

Interesting. This conversation was the first time Ramona mentioned having a sister. So, I couldn't help wondering what else Ramona might've kept from me.

I whipped my wand out, then pointed it at Ramona. "Firio!"

A sea of red, orange, and yellow spat out from my wand and onto the ground before jumping towards Ramona.

"I'm not afraid of fire." She grabbed her wand and faced the flickering flames. "Waterio."

Water oozed out of her wand and extinguished the fire in a matter of seconds.

"Vinesio," Ramona squeaked.

Four vines spurted out of Ramona's wand and tied themselves around each one of my limbs.

Sweat tumbled down my back. I tried breaking free while the vines wrapped themselves tighter and tighter around my arms and legs. This couldn't be it. I was only twelve years old. I couldn't die now. I hadn't even told Enzo how I felt about him. Because there was a truth nobody knew about me. Both boys and girls intrigued me.

Fire might have been too dangerous for my arms because I didn't want to risk burning myself. But I could recover from the cold.

"Icio!" I summoned all the energy I had while concentrating on the vine wrapped around my left arm. Ice oozed out of the wand, and landed on the vine I intended it to. The vine disintegrated as the ice traveled to the rest of the vines.

But I didn't wait around to exchange more banter with Ramona.

So, I ran out the front door. In fact, I was in such a hurry that I didn't have time to think about how Father would have been furious at me for slamming the door. Now wasn't the time to be concerned with decorum.

I scurried down the steps. Then I checked my right arm, making sure I still had my wand. Because it didn't matter where I was. I would always worry.

I almost turned left out of my dirt driveway when footsteps pounded against the ground.

Someone snickered. "You didn't think you'd get away that easily, did you?"

I whipped my body around. It was Ramona.

"Water, water, water, make me a river and trap my stepmother," I chanted.

Rushing water bounced through the air. Ramona gasped, then lost her balance, falling into the river in my dirt driveway.

I turned left before trekking down the street. Wind ripped through the air, slapping my cheeks.

I huffed while picking up my pace.

Going on a quest wasn't what I should've been doing—I was only a kid. Yet I didn't have a choice. Life didn't care how I thought it was unfair. Defeating Ramona was what I had to do. And I also had to think about Mother and Father. Their opinion of me mattered despite how they were no longer alive. Wanting to make them proud was only natural. And that meant not giving up, no matter how daunting life seemed. If I escaped Ramona, then I might've had a chance to fetch the crystal from the Kuku Mountains.

Birds screeched through the cloudless sky sometime later while dozens of trees stood in front of me. A **WELCOME TO WHIMSY** sign soon caught my attention.

Marino's deal might not have been ideal, but it was all I had. So, I'd put my pride and frustration aside and start the journey.

Someone tapped my back, and I shrieked. No explanation was necessary how worrying about Ramona catching up to me was a natural reaction. She was an adult whereas I was a kid. So, there was a chance that she'd eventually overpower me.

I spun around. Enzo stood in front of me—not Ramona.

So, yeah. If Ramona hadn't found me yet, then I might've stood a chance of completing my mission.

My cheeks flushed. "What are you doing here?"

He crossed his arms. "Where do you think you're going?"

My back hairs rose while contempt radiated from his eyes. I might not have been dealing with Ramona, but I was gonna have to think of something fast. It didn't matter if Enzo and I were best friends. Nothing would keep me from retrieving the crystal from the Kuku Mountains. It was a promise.

5

A TRAVEL COMPANION

"You didn't answer my question, Enzo," I said moments later, glaring at him.

Anger continued flaring through my body. Sure. Enzo might have been my best friend. And I had my secret crush on him. But he wasn't the boss of me. Plus, it was kind of odd that he kept tabs on me.

Enzo cocked an eyebrow. "I was worried about you. I saw the scuffle with your stepmother. Besides, you didn't tell me how the meeting with Marino the Great went."

Rays of sunlight radiated from the sky, making me wipe a few beads of sweat from my face. Rambling would have meant dwelling on how the temperatures were surprisingly warm for this time of year. But no. Enzo still hadn't gotten to the point. Besides, Ramona could appear at any second.

"I was right about Ramona trying to kill me, and we had a confrontation," I blurted.

Enzo gaped. "I'm so sorry."

"Thanks."

"You're sure this isn't a misunderstanding?"

He might have meant well, but he should have known better than to ask a stupid question. The time for believing the best in Ramona was over. She tried to kill me, and no amount of optimism would change that fact. The sooner I accepted the truth about my stepfather, the sooner my life would return to normal.

"Why?" I asked. "Because I have an overactive imagination?"

Enzo nibbled on the inside of his lip. "Don't put words in my mouth. I just meant things sometimes look worse than they are."

I shook my head vigorously. "It doesn't get much clearer than confessing and using magic to try and kill me."

"Fine. You're right."

Enzo was smart for not arguing with me. Continuing to doubt my honesty would have made me scream and stomp my feet on the ground. Making him believe how Ramona almost killed me wasn't my job. Being my best friend meant he should have given me the benefit of the doubt. I was the one who always supported him when he and his sister Hanna argued, which was at least two or three times a week.

I forced a grin. "If you'll excuse me, I have to go."

Enzo's gaze shifted to the **WELCOME TO WHIMSY** sign. Then he glanced back at me. "Wait? You agreed to Marino the Great's deal?"

Tears dotted my eyes despite how Father would have told me not to get so overwhelmed by emotions. Because I couldn't help myself. Running away from home should have been the last thing on my mind. I was a kid, and shouldn't have had to make a deal with a magician to solve my problems.

"You don't understand," I said.

"Make me, Alex."

"I can't go back to Ramona."

"I never said you should," Enzo said.

"Then what are you saying?" I asked.

Enzo coughed into his arm. "You still haven't told me why she tried to kill you."

Getting flustered would have been fair if someone besides Enzo asked me that question. But I couldn't get too mad at Enzo. Whether I accepted the truth or not, Enzo was the only person in my life I could count on. So, I needed to do my best to remain patient with him. I didn't know what I'd do if I lost Enzo. I could only handle so much disappointment before cracking.

My jaw trembled. "My father left me his rubies. And Ramona is angry because she can only get them if I die."

Enzo snickered. "Why would he leave the rubies to you? No offense, or anything, but you're not eighteen yet."

I shrugged. "The point is, he did."

"No need to get defensive. It was just a question."

The wind howled even louder, slapping against my face.

"Anyway, I have no qualms about the deal I made. It's the only way to get rid of Ramona for good," I revealed.

Enzo scratched the side of his head. "And you trust him?"

"He doesn't have a reason to double-cross me—he wants to see his dead wife."

"But nobody from Flimsy has ever gone to Whimsy before. At least in a very long time."

I rolled my eyes. "It's not like the Queen will have me arrested."

My comment was true. Getting in trouble for traveling seemed like the dumbest thing in the world. It wasn't like I was selling Flimsy secrets to an enemy country. Although Enzo still had every time to be shocked because Flimsy and Whimsy never interacted with each other.

I sucked in a breath. "I've made up my mind, Enzo."

"I can see that."

I averted my gaze. Sure. Making the deal with Marino the Great and traveling to Whimsy had to be done. But pangs of nostalgia would roll through my body. Leaving my best friend behind would be difficult.

I gave him a pleading look. "Please don't say anything to Ramona..."

"Forget about Ramona for a second. I'm going with you, and there's nothing you can do to stop me."

"You can't go with me. Hanna will be furious."

Enzo grabbed my hand, giving it a quick squeeze. "I don't care. You'll need someone to keep you on task. Besides, I would be a terrible best friend if I let you go alone."

There it was again. An example of Enzo's odd behavior. Because I wanted nothing more than to shake my head at Enzo, holding my hand. But that was only a superfluous distraction. I hadn't begun my mission, and wouldn't find the Kuku mountains by talking to Enzo all day.

My heart fluttered. "Fine."

An elk darted to the ground in the distance, leaves crunching under its feet. It then disappeared after a beat.

Enzo smiled. "Great. Where do we begin?"

6

PEGASUS THE PEACOCK

"It'd be nice to take a break," Enzo said sometime later while we continued walking through the maze of trees after crossing the border into Whimsy.

I scoffed. "No offense or anything, but you know what you signed up for."

"I know, I know. But it's not just my feet. Look up at the sky." Enzo pointed above.

Yup. Enzo might have been annoying, but he wasn't an idiot. The sky was a mixture of blue and black, with more black than blue. Although I didn't want to think about how it was almost nighttime, because it didn't matter how old I was. I always cringed at darkness because something terrifying always existed about the unknown.

I huffed. "Fine. What do you wanna do?"

"We should set up camp."

"We didn't bring any supplies," I said.

Enzo sniggered. "It doesn't matter. We have our wands."

"Okay. Let's set up camp." I pointed my wand. "Land, oh, land, gift us with a tent and two sleeping bags."

Nothing appeared.

"Land, oh, land, gift us with a tent and two sleeping bags."

Ficklewamper. Enzo and I were once again out of luck, which seemed odd. I couldn't think of a reason for our wands not to work.

Enzo sighed. "Let me try. Land, oh, land, please gift us with a tent and two sleeping bags."

Ficklewamper. Nothing happened.

An itch shot up my chin, and I scratched it. "Maybe our wands are broken."

"That's doubtful," Enzo said.

"You don't know that. Father was always having to replace his wand."

Enzo scowled. "Not now, Alex. We have to figure out what to do."

A popping sound echoed before a mist the size of a couple of adult men appeared and masked the air and ground in front of us. The fog disappeared a moment later, revealing a bird, which was about the height of Enzo.

Hmmm. The word for the type of bird standing in front of us escaped me, even though I should have known the answer. I was the one who read every book I found, which meant I must have come across the bird before. I just didn't know where. And that was a big problem because there was nothing more annoying than having words escape me. I of all people, should have realized that point since Grandma used to always complain about words escaping her when she was alive.

Enzo bowed, which seemed formal, but now was no time to criticize him. "You're a pretty peacock."

Ficklewamper. Peacock was the word I wanted to use, yet it slipped my mind. Hopefully, that wasn't indicative of more serious memory problems.

"Thank you," screeched the peacock, making me cover my ears. Yup, the noise was comparable to nails on a chalkboard.

"Our wands aren't working...do you think they would be broken?" I asked.

Enzo snorted at me. "Ficklewamper. Ficklewamper. Ficklewamper. I already told you they aren't broken, Alex. You're just too stubborn to listen to me."

Okay, Enzo. Excuse me for wanting confirmation. If there was a chance that the peacock might have been able to help us, then that was good. Or perhaps I was relieved that the peacock wasn't attacking us.

The peacock bobbed its head. "Your friend is right. Wands don't work in Whimsy."

I gasped. "Excuse me?"

The peacock flapped its fanned tail against the ground before it floated in midair above us. "Magic is a peculiar thing here."

I shook my head. "What do you mean? Our wands must be broken if they don't work."

"I stand by what I said," replied the peacock.

Insisting the wands were broken had nothing to do with being stubborn. I wasn't. However, it still would have been nice if the peacock gave us a clear answer. Having my head explode from confusion was the last thing I needed.

"Believing is all that is required for magic in Whimsy," the peacock continued.

My lips curled. "What do you mean?"

"Maybe I should ask the questions," Enzo interrupted.

"Don't be absurd," I snapped, annoyance flickering through me. "I'm perfectly able to talk to the peacock. Anyway, what's your name?"

"I'm Pegasus," said the peacock.

Pegasus the peacock? That was quite the mouthful.

Enzo put his hands in his jacket pockets. "Go back to the part about believing. What did you mean?"

"If you want something to appear, just think about it enough," the peacock said.

Enzo quirked an eyebrow. "Are you saying magic is like wish fulfillment here?"

The peacock cackled. "Sure. Let's go with that."

"Did you appear here to help us?" I asked.

Enzo smacked his hand over his head. "Don't be ridiculous, Alex. The peacock isn't gonna help us."

"The name's Pegasus, in case you've forgotten," added the peacock. "And if you have, maybe you need to get your memory checked. But your friend is once again right. I follow my whims and disappear and appear at a moment's notice. Now if you'll excuse me, I must be going. I have a very invigorating conference to get to."

The force from the popping sound echoing through the air was almost enough to make Enzo and me fall backwards. But no. We somehow managed to keep standing. The peacock then disappeared into a funnel fog since it was gone the moment the mist clear.

I grunted. "You didn't need to second guess me."

"You were the one asking stupid questions."

"There's no such thing as a stupid question."

"Then maybe you haven't been paying attention enough in school," Enzo spat.

I crossed my arms. "You shouldn't have come with me if you were gonna second guess me."

He looped his arms around me, then stared me down. "Let's not argue. It's been a long day for both of us. Me with Hanna and you with Ramona."

Enzo could say that again. I didn't even want to think about how I was supposed to get to sleep tonight. Saying my stepmother tried to kill me to fuel her own greed wasn't something I should have contemplated. Dealing with that type of person resembled something from one of those fables Mom used to read to me at bedtime when she was alive.

Sure. A conniving stepmother might have made for an interesting story. But enduring betrayal was enough to make me shout, "ficklewamper" several more times. We hadn't had the stereotypical bad relationship that most children might have expected to have with his or her stepparent.

Enzo shifted his gaze before making a tent appear on the ground before us. The tent sprung up in front of us, which was great. Spending time assembling it was the last thing I needed to do after a long day.

My stomach knotted. "I do appreciate you coming here, Enzo."

"I know, I know. No need for formalities."

I sniggered. The image of Enzo bowing before the peacock wasn't something I would forget anytime soon.

It was just a bird as opposed to a king or queen, and one would think that wouldn't be necessary.

Something hooted, then I shrieked.

"Calm down. It's just an owl." Enzo patted my shoulder, letting his hand linger for a beat longer than it should have. And I would've debated Enzo's intentions if I felt like being analytical. But I didn't. Not after my long day.

I titled my head. He was right because the faint outline of an owl resting on a branch of a nearby tree was visible.

"What should we do with the wands?" I asked.

"I'll take care of them," called out a voice.

Enzo and I whirled around, only to be greeted by Pegasus. The peacock strutted over to us and yanked my wand from my hand before snapping it in half with his beak. He then did the same thing to Enzo's wand.

I squealed at Pegasus. "We might need them later when we return to Flimsy."

"Nobody ever leaves Whimsy," Pegasus said.

I swallowed the lump in my throat. "Are you serious?"

"I don't know. You tell me," Pegasus replied.

Enzo's eyes bulged up. "What made you return to us?"

"My conference wasn't as interesting as I thought it would be. Anyway, see you around/" Pegasus disappeared as quickly as arriving.

I jabbed my fists through the air. "Pegasus had no right to break our wands, Enzo. Oh, maybe I made a big mistake by coming here."

"We can always get new wands."

"I guess. But I still think Pegasus is more than a little sneaky."

He laughed. "Yeah, I agree with you."

"It's not funny," I said.

He tugged at the sides of his jacket. "It's important to have a sense of humor, Alex."

Fair enough. But doing so was easier said than done. I wasn't supposed to jump for joy because a stupid talking peacock broke our wands.

"You don't think something bad will happen to us when we leave Whimsy, do you?" I stammered."

"You should go with your gut."

I frowned. "And what's that supposed to mean?"

He coughed into his arm. "Pegasus probably said that to upset you."

"Well, he succeeded."

I glanced at my hands, then gritted my teeth. The man's map was no longer in my possession. Ficklewamper. Losing the map was something else I also needed. NOT.

"Calm down. I have it." Enzo handed the map to me.

I pouted after studying the map for a beat. "I might as well have lost it. It's just an outline of Whimsy with nothing else but a red X on the other side of the country. It's useless, I tell you."

Enzo rubbed my back for a beat. "Let's just go to bed. I'm sure everything will seem less upsetting in the morning."

I didn't know whether to smile or cry. On the one hand, I was thankful Enzo tried cheering me up. Yet I hoped he wasn't just telling me what I wanted to hear. If someone was gonna tell me something disappointing, then Enzo was the one to do it. That was his prerogative as my best friend, after all.

"It better," I finally said.

Wind whistled, stinging my face. So much for the warm temperatures—we definitely weren't in Flimsy anymore.

7

MORE PEACOCK ANTICS

Sunlight snuck through my tent the following morning before I yawned and rubbed my eyes. I then tilted my head. Enzo wasn't in his sleeping bag.

Hmmm. It would have been a shame if something bad happened to him. Like Pegasus the peacock sneaking into the tent in the middle of the night and dragging Enzo off to an awful place. But I was probably wrong and everything would be fine because I had no idea what I would do if one more thing went wrong.

I exited the tent. A wooden table with a bench on both sides with two plates of waffles, a bottle of syrup, two bowls of blueberries, two cups of water, and a tray with a stick of butter. There was also a place mat under both of the plates, which were across from each other on the table, and a napkin with a fork, knife, and a spoon resting on it.

Enzo stood, then shuffled over to me. "I thought you'd never wake up."

"You could've woken me up."

"I was letting you sleep in."

I gave him a small smile. "Thank you. That was kind of you."

"I thought you could use the rest after a stressful day," Enzo said.

I raised an eyebrow. "Where did you get all this stuff?"

"I used magic," Enzo mumbled.

I put my hands on my hips. "What do you mean? How is that possible?"

Enzo clenched his jaw. "I just believed it was. I took Pegasus's advice."

"Don't even mention that maniac. I never want to see him again."

He snickered. "Whatever you say, Alex."

"It's not funny. I'm still fuming because he broke our wands."

"We'll be fine without our wands."

I rolled my eyes. "You don't know that."

"It's important to have faith. Now come on. Let's eat before our food gets cold." Enzo guided me to the wooden table, and I sat on the side closet to us while he took the side opposite me.

I sipped some water before speaking. "This was really kind of you Enzo."

"Don't mention it. I know blueberries and waffles are your favorite food. Besides, it's my job to take care of you."

Guilt panged through my body despite how I didn't do anything too bad. That was the problem with rambling. It made a person think about everything, which in this case meant considering how I should have had a better attitude yesterday.

He lifted his gaze off his plate. "You should eat your food."

"I know, I know." I reached for the syrup and splattered a more than generous portion on the side of my plate before grabbing the butter and plopping two slices down on my waffles.

"Do you like the food?" Enzo asked.

"It's nice." I finished the piece of waffle in my mouth, reaching for another sip of water.

He extended his hand, touching mine. "I know things seem difficult, but try not to be upset. You always have me."

There it was again. The thing that made me wanna pinch myself. Being friends with someone was one thing. But it was another to feel the need to always emphasize the friendship's closeness. And no. I wasn't imagining things. I never once saw or heard friends talk to each other the way Enzo always talked to me. Staring at Enzo wasn't a good idea, though, even if I couldn't help drooling at his short spiked up black hair. But I once again stood by something I said earlier, since I had done nothing bad. People had crushes all the time, since it was a part of growing up. The important thing was not to act on those feelings. Nothing would have been worse than ruining my friendship with Enzo. Except maybe seeing Ramona again. But that was a problem for another day.

He bit his lip. "Something wrong?"

I whipped my head back and forth in a vigorous fashion. "No. Everything is perfect."

"I can think of something wrong," screeched a voice. "You didn't invite me to your party. Although it's blasphemous to use magic to make food appear. Even peasants don't do that. Although that might be because they don't know how to."

I shifted my gaze, then nausea washed over me. Pegasus the peacock was the last thing Enzo and I needed to deal with. After all, it wasn't unreasonable to want a few moments of peace.

Pegasus strutted over to the table. Then I stood.

Being calm might have been a nice idea. But this was real life, and problems couldn't be compartmentalized into neat categories. Every ounce of rage shooting through my body was justified. It would have been one thing if Pegasus was helpful. But he hadn't been. He just liked wasting our time. In fact, if I didn't know any better, then I would have thought he enjoyed taunting us.

Taunting. It was an interesting word. Sure. The description might have been a little harsh. But it was the only word that came to mind.

Maybe, just maybe, there was a chance I could use magic. I might not have been perfect, but I wasn't thick. I believed in magic and it would be nice if I could have summoned some fire to make Pegasus leave us alone.

"Why so tense?" Pegasus asked.

"Seeing you wasn't on my agenda," I said.

"I'm only trying to help." Pegasus expanded his tail so it once again resumed the shape of a fan.

I glared at him. "You have a funny way of showing it."

A tingling sensation jolted my body. All the clouds were now stacked together, in addition to being a saturated gray color. Snow was also crashing down from the sky.

Pegasus giggled. "I bet you're shocked by the snow."

"Don't read my mind," I spat.

"Calm down," Pegasus said. "I wasn't reading your mind. It was just obvious from your facial expression. You should work on hiding your emotions. But don't get mad at the weather. It makes Whimsy beautiful since the weather changes on a moment's notice."

"That's it! I've had it." My screams echoed through the air, making a nearby deer scurry away. The image of an ember formed in my mind before multiplying and turning into a full-blown fire. A sea of red, orange, and yellow then spat out of both of my hands and dropped on the ground before shooting towards Pegasus and making him step backwards.

"That was close," Pegasus screeched. "You could have burned me."

"That was the idea," I said.

Enzo got up from the table and walked over to me before shooting a gaze at Pegasus. "Perhaps you should go. You aren't wanted here."

Pegasus smacked his tail against the ground before floating in midair. "But the fun hasn't even begun."

Enzo drew in a breath. "Perhaps we could poof to the Kuku mountains and retrieve the crystal. Then all of our problems would be over."

"I'm afraid you can't do that," Pegasus interrupted.

My jaw lowered. "Excuse me?"

"Whimsy doesn't have many laws," Pegasus revealed. "But it's important to follow the ones that do exist. Law 504 says foreigners are not allowed to poof places. There's even an anti-vaporizing enchantment so that only Whimsy citizens can poof places. But go ahead. Try and break the enchantment. I dare you."

The scorching sensation returned to my stomach. There was nothing more I would have loved than to blast Pegasus to the other side of Whimsy. Although that wouldn't have done much, because Enzo and I needed to go to the other side of Whimsy to retrieve the crystal.

I wasn't unreasonable because of being irritated by Pegasus. What he just said confirmed my opinion about him. He didn't only like having a good time. He was a troublemaker because it almost seemed like he was trying to goad us into getting into trouble. Well, no offense to the vimplepimper of a peacock, but I wasn't that dumb.

And yup. I said vimplepimper even though that was a worse word than ficklewamper. It wasn't like I went around telling kids younger than me that they should use foul language. I just sometimes used it myself. And it wasn't even because I thought it made me look cool. It was just that intense situations required intense emotions. It was that simple.

Enzo winced. "What would happen if someone broke the law, and was able to lift the enchantment?"

"The person might lose his or her head or get a lifetime in solitary confinement," Pegasus revealed.

"That's terrible," I said.

"What do you expect?" Pegasus asked. "Whimsy needs to defend itself from Flimsy."

I folded my arms. "What do you mean?"

"Forget it," Pegasus chirped. "It's not important. You can learn about the history of Whimsy and Flimsy some other day. The important thing is that help will always be offered to those who need it in Whimsy."

I frowned at Pegasus. "What are you talking about?"

"Whimsy prides itself on being a generous country. But you don't have to take my word for it. See for yourself." Pegasus turned his head. A door floated in the air that Enzo or I could reach. It was less than a foot above us.

"Why should we trust you?" I asked.

Pegasus remained silent for a moment. "Because Whimsy really is a generous country. Sticking around long enough will prove I'm right."

I scoffed. There was no way that blasted peacock would ever be right about anything. But now wasn't the time to do anything about it.

"Go on," Pegasus said. "What's the worst that could happen?"

I pursed my lips. "We could die."

"That's doubtful," Pegasus said. "I stand by my original statement. Help will always be offered to those who need it."

"What about cleaning up the food and tent and sleeping bags?" I asked.

"I'll take care of it." Enzo stared at his right index finger and thumb before snapping them. The table and tent were gone now-as if we never had a nice breakfast or slept in this part of the woods in the first place.

I turned to Enzo. "What do you think we should do?"

"We should try the door," Enzo said.

I nodded at him. "Okay. I trust you."

Enzo took my hand, then guided me to the door before opening it.

"This is the most bizarre thing I've seen so far in Whimsy. It's just more sky." I peeked through the door while still making sure to have my feet on the grass because I didn't quite know what would happen.

Enzo clicked his lips. "You're right, Alex. Maybe this door isn't going to help us after all."

"Don't be bashful. Don't you know life is more fun when you live it on the edge a little?" Pegasus poked my back with his beak, making me fall through the door.

I did the only thing I could. I yelled while closing my eyes.

Sure. Some people might have preferred to know what would happen. But not me. Cluelessness was better in this case because knowledge wasn't always power. It sometimes made things worse. It was a fact.

8

MULTIPLIER BEES

"Alex!" Enzo screamed.

I thudded against something a moment later before opening my eyes. I stood on a hill overlooking a body of water. Although at least there weren't any waves right now. Because more trouble was the last thing I wanted or needed.

That blasted peacock. Pegasus just had to push us. The worst part was he was right. Nothing bad happened to me since I was still alive. However, I would never admit my relief to the peacock. Being correct would have gone to his head.

Something thumped, and I scooted a few feet behind me before offering my hand and pulling Enzo up from the ground.

Wow. I had been so distracted with my internal rambling that I hadn't seen Enzo plummeting to his almost death. So, yeah. Maybe I would have to start paying more attention. That was a goal for another day, though, because I had no idea where we were right now.

Something crackled, revealing a cloud of fog before Pegasus the peacock appeared in midair in front of us.

"I told you would be okay," Pegasus said.

I pointed my finger at Pegasus. "You pushed us out the door."

"You should thank me," Pegasus said. "Your life just got more exciting."

"You admit you pushed us?" I wiped sweat from my forehead.

Pegasus nodded. "Yes. I pushed you."

I yelled louder this time. "How could you do that?"

"Do what?" asked Pegasus.

"Push us—we could have been hurt," I said, stuttering.

Pegasus's eyes widened. "I didn't admit to pushing you."

"You just did," I said.

Pegasus cackled. "I did no such thing. Or maybe I did. My memory isn't what it used to be."

Ficklewamper. Arguing with the blasted peacock was pointless because being direct didn't seem to be his strong suit.

Something buzzed behind me, making me flinch. Although it was only a bee.

Okay. A bee might not have been my favorite thing in the world. But a bee wasn't the worst thing in the world compared to everything else that happened over the last day.

The bee continued buzzing while flying near my face. I kept swatting it and swatting it while closing my eyes. Being honest meant admitting I had a fear of bees, even if things could have been a lot worse. But the bee just flew to a new part of my face. Although something strange happened because the buzzing seemed louder now than when the bee first appeared. Almost like the sound of thousands of trumpets.

I opened my eyes. My heart thumped louder and faster, fear radiating through my body. There were now hundreds, if not thousands, of bees swarming within inches of me.

"You shouldn't have been swatting the bees," Pegasus said.

I quirked an eyebrow. "Do I even want to ask?"

"They're multiplier bees. They multiply each time someone swats them. It's genius if you ask me," Pegasus said.

"Nobody asked you," I interrupted.

Yeah. I had no qualms about being rude to Pegasus. Pegasus deserved it since he caused me more than a little irritation.

I cracked my knuckles. "We're going to die, Enzo. I just know it."

"That might be true in this case," Pegasus said. "Multiplier bee venom is deadly. But they almost never sting."

More sweat dripped down my back. "What do we do, Enzo?"

"The only option is down," Pegasus said.

I gave the peacock a dirty look. "I wasn't talking to you."

"That's okay. I felt like sharing." Pegasus disappeared into a funnel of fog, which was good. There was no telling what I'd do to the peacock if his antics escalated.

The bees inched a little closer to us while Enzo grabbed my hand. "Do you trust me?" he asked.

I didn't even have to think about my answer. "Absolutely."

Enzo pointed to a boat below us as the thin silhouette of a man with a hook, tailcoat jacket, pants, boots, and an eye patch was visible-even from a distance. Or maybe I just had good vision.

"We're gonna fly and land on the boat below us," Enzo said.

I pouted. "We could land in the water and die."

Enzo gave me a dirty look. "I thought you trusted me?"

"I do trust you. It's Whimsy I don't trust."

The bees pivoted in the air; stingers were now visible. They soon started closing the distance between us.

"It's now or never." Enzo squeezed my hand even tighter while he leaped off the hill, and I closed my eyes.

"Are we dead yet, Enzo?"

"Open your eyes and see for yourself."

I did as Enzo instructed. Somehow, we were actually flying.

"I don't believe it!" I exclaimed. "It's a miracle."

"I told you to trust me."

We landed in the boat after another beat. Although Enzo should have done a better job with landing because we thudded against the boat.

"What the blazes is going on?" said a hoarse voice.

Glancing at the man was enough to confirm my initial thought from the cliff. He had to have been a pirate. Asking my honest opinion also meant admitting he needed a haircut. His voluminous hair extended to his shoulders.

Enzo pressed his hands together. "You have to take us to shore, sir. We just narrowly avoided getting stung by multiplier bees."

The man chuckled at us. "Then why didn't you say so? There's nothing I wouldn't do for women or children. I used to have a wife and son but they got eaten by Carlyle the Kraken many moons ago. Although that's a story for another day. By the looks on your faces, I say you have enough problems already."

Okay. Good to know I wasn't the only one with a complicated past. And I would have even asked him to elaborate on what he was talking about. But the man was correct. My pulse still rang in my ear while sweat clung to my forehead.

I snorted. "That's the understatement of the century."

Enzo's eyes lit up. "Are you a pirate?"

"Former pirate," he said. "I'm reformed, and only do good things now. Anyway, the name's Francis."

"I'm Enzo." Enzo pointed to me. "And this is Alex."

Something smashed against the water, which splashed us a little. Ficklewamper. Whatever. No use in complaining about a little water.

Enzo's lips quivered. "What was that?"

Wow. Maybe Enzo spent too much time hanging out with me, since he was now worried.

"I want you too to remain calm," Francis said. "But we have a slight problem."

I craned my head, then screamed. A creature with a purple circular head the size of several adult grown men with bright red eyes was behind us. It also had a giant x under its left eyes.

"Is that Carlyle?" I asked.

"Yes. And this is going to be a bumpy ride." Francis walked over to the motor and yanked the string just as Carlyle lifted one of its tentacles out of the water.

The boat lunged forward several thousand feet in a matter of seconds. I fell backwards and onto Enzo, who was on the motorboat's floor.

"I'm sorry." I stood.

Enzo brushed the dust off him. "Don't worry about it."

Enzo and I fell down again as the boat jerked forward again.

"You two should probably just stay on the floor till we get to the docks at the other end of Lake Whim. Carlyle is still behind us. Also, sorry for not warning you about just how fast the boat is," Francis said, as his voice almost audible over the engine's roaring.

The motor boat continued banging against the water while the clunky engine echoed.

I almost pulled my hair out. Going off on a tangent meant realizing Pegasus the peacock was once against right. Help had once again been offered to us, even if it was unexpected.

I still loathed saying one nice thing about the blasted peacock, though. We wouldn't have been in the multiplier bee or kraken predicament in the first place if he hadn't pushed me through the door.

Whatever. What was done was done. I would just have to hope I didn't run into Pegasus again. Or if I did, I wouldn't trust another word that came out of his vile mouth. And no. Using the word vile didn't make me dramatic. It made me practical because Pegasus should have been ashamed of himself after all the trouble he caused.

I grunted.

It was probably a safe bet Pegasus had never felt one ounce of shame in his life before.

"You can get up now," Francis said.

Enzo and I stood. And sure enough, Francis was right. The boat was tied to the docks.

I grinned at Francis. "Thank you for helping us."

"My pleasure," Francis said.

"Are you sure you don't want to come with us?" I asked. "Enzo and I could use a smart person like yourself."

Enzo rubbed his forehead.

Francis sighed. "That's very kind of you, but I can't. Now that you two are safe, I must resume my crusade against Carlyle, because I'm not going to bed tonight till either him or me is dead."

My back hairs pricked up.

So much for thinking I was the only dramatic person, because I wasn't. Blaming Francis for his blood feud with Carlyle would have been unfair, since anyone would have been mad about losing a spouse and kid.

"We should get going." Enzo tugged at my arm.

"Thanks again, Francis," I said before following Enzo's lead and stepping foot onto the docks.

Francis undid the motor boat's connection to the dock before starting the engine and blasting off into the distance. Whatever. I did all I could because I was polite and thanked him. Although hopefully he wouldn't meet his doom today.

9

THE SIRENS

"This has really turned into a terrible day, Enzo," I said while we continued standing on the docks. "We could have died three times already."

"I wish you wouldn't be negative."

Being negative couldn't be helped, no matter how much thought I gave the matter. Going off on tangents had nothing to do with the issue. I challenged anyone not to be a little perplexed by almost being killed three times today. It was only morning, which made the whole situation worse.

Enzo picked at his nail. "At least Francis helped us."

"Yes, that was good."

"Why are you always so negative, Alex?"

I shrugged. "I don't know. It must be because I lost both of my parents."

"I did too, and I'm not negative."

"I can't change who I am."

"I wasn't asking you to."

The trees shook while the wind howled, making me rub my arms together. Ficklewamper. I must have left my jacket back in the tent. Either that, or I forgot to take one with me in the first place when I left Ramona's yesterday afternoon.

"Here you can take mine." Enzo removed his jacket and placed it on me, electrifying every cell in my body.

Although the static from his touch was almost enough to make me recoil. Sure. There was a difference between being shocked by something and being struck by lightning. But it was still unexpected.

"That was nice of you to leap to your almost doom," I said.

"I'd do anything for you."

There it was again. Enzo saying something someone who was only a friend wouldn't say. And no. I wasn't reading too much into things. I couldn't help myself since I always picked up on the little things. It must have been because I wanted to be a writer. Authors had to notice people's little quirks, otherwise they wouldn't have any fodder to write about.

"Did you ever think we would be off on some sort of adventure?" I asked.

Enzo chuckled. "Don't shoot me, but I did."

Okay. I had a reason to laugh. My dramatic tendencies were starting to rub off on Enzo if he was making intense statements. But I could admit when Enzo was right because doing so was different than saying Pegasus was right about something. One would expect a rambler to get lost on some sort of adventure. Perhaps Whimsy wasn't even as bad as I thought it was regardless of Pegasus, the random door, the multiplier bees, and Carlyle the Kraken. Every second that I spent in Whimsy was one less I didn't have to spend thinking about going back to Flimsy and facing Ramona. Sure. Marino the Great might have agreed to help me. But there were a million other things that would have been nicer to do than face off against Ramona.

He winked. "What are you thinking about?"

"Nothing. It's not important."

"I'll be the judge of that."

"Where's the map and necklace?" I asked.

Being dishonest might have been the nicest thing in the world. And I usually loathed the idea of telling a lie. But annoying Enzo and going off on a ramble about my worries was the last thing I wanted to do right now.

"In my right coat pocket," Enzo said.

I unzipped the right coat pocket and put my hand in it, only to sigh. Enzo was right. I then zipped the pocket up.

"What do we do now?" Enzo asked.

"There's something I have to tell you," I said.

Enzo elevated an eyebrow. "Is it bad?"

"No. But it's important."

"Okay. Go ahead. You know you can tell me anything."

Telling Enzo about my small crush on him might have been dangerous. But I didn't have a choice. I'd never know how Enzo would feel about me until I was honest. And the issue was less complicated than I realized. He'd either reciprocate my feelings or he'd reject me, and I'd have to move on. But either way, I'd have an answer.

"I can sometimes be a little confused," I said.

"What do we have here?" called out a voice.

"I don't know, sis, but they look good prey," said a second person.

Enzo and I shifted our bodies. Blonde-haired women sporting black dresses stood before us.

"Stay behind me, Alex." Enzo stepped in front of me, expanding his arms.

The woman that spoke first cackled. "How cute. You're defending your friend. But it's a shame we have to end you."

"What are you talking about?" I asked.

The second woman flipped her hair over her shoulders. "Maybe we should tell them, Maggie."

Maggie nodded. "I agree, Sophie."

"We're sirens," Maggie said.

Sirens. It was an interesting word because it didn't matter if I was in Flimsy or Whimsy. Sirens existed in Flimsy too. Although I had never seen one. But I was privy to plenty of stories and knew what they were and what they did.

"We have to get out of here," I whispered.

"What was that?" Sophie asked. "Don't you know it's rude to mumble? You should speak up so my sister and I can hear you."

Maggie sneered. "Enough chatting. Let's get on with it."

Sophie sighed at her sister. "If you insist."

They both started staring at us from their current position a few feet away. Nothing happened since Enzo and I remained right where we were.

Maggie shrilled. "I don't understand. They should be sliding toward us."

"Perhaps we should walk over to them," Sophie suggested.

My heart pounded a little faster inside my chest because having two sirens walk over to me was the last thing I wanted or needed.

Maggie and Sophie darted over to us.

Maggie yanked me away from Enzo before pressing her bright red lips against my forehead. But nothing bad happened since I didn't feel any pain right now. At least for me. Maggie screamed while she started liquefying before splattering onto the ground.

"I'm melting!" Maggie screamed.

"Me too!" Sophie yelled.

Maggie and Sophie were now just water on the docks. The two separate blobs of water constricted before nothing was left of Maggie or Sophie. Well, two black dresses were left. But that was only a small detail.

I clapped my hand over my mouth. "I can't believe it! Something went right. The sirens couldn't suck our souls and melted."

Enzo nudged my shoulder. "I told you need to be a little more optimistic."

"Yeah, yeah, yeah."

"You learned an important lesson."

My eyes bulged up. But there was nothing menacing about my expression. It was a mocking nature as opposed to a malicious nature. "And what would that be?"

Enzo winked. "That I am always right."

I laughed. "Yeah, okay. Whatever you say."

"I'm serious."

"I'm sure you are."

Someone's back became visible out of the corner of my eyes. I bit my lip because I would have recognized the goldish-red tinted hair anywhere. It was Enzo's older sister Hanna.

"What's wrong?" Enzo asked.

I leaned into his right ear. "Hanna's here, and we have to leave now."

There was a door in front of us, which meant we could go through it. Or maybe it just appeared now since Whimsy prided itself on always helping people. According to Pegasus, that was. Because he didn't have much credibility.

I opened the door before closing my eyes and stepping through it. Enzo followed behind me, and a crunching noise echoed after a beat.

I opened my eyes, realizing we fell on a pile of leaves, which was a mixture of red, orange, and yellow. Turning my attention back towards the direction of the door made me realize it was now gone.

Whatever. Waiting till later to understand Whimsy logic was for the best. I didn't want my head to explode. Because Enzo and I just avoided death for the fourth time in less than 24 hours.

I scratched my head. "Don't tell me we're back where we started."

"No, I don't think so," Enzo said, pointing. "The leaves still on the tree are blue and the leaves back in the woods we started in that were still on the trees were green."

Wow. Blue leaves on the trees and orange, red, and yellow leaves on the ground. Yeah. That didn't make a lot of sense. But I couldn't be surprised. Logic still wasn't Whimsy's strong suit.

Although at least Enzo and I outwitted the sirens. Sometimes, appreciating a small victory was a person's only option. Enzo and I were still alive, and that fact counted for something. We could've died. Yet we didn't. Perhaps life wasn't all terrible.

10

HANNA'S ARRIVAL

"How are you doing, my friends?" called out a voice.

I didn't need to spin around to know who arrived. I would have recognized the screeching anywhere, because there was only one voice that would have made so much rage flash through my body.

"What do you want, Pegasus?" I asked.

Pegasus strutted over to us. "I wanted to see how my two-favorite people were doing."

I gave the blasted peacock a dirty look. "Like you care."

"I care a lot," Pegasus said. "Or perhaps not at all. That's for you to decide, child."

I rolled up my sleeves. "We fell through another door, and then the door disappeared. Why is that?"

"You could at least ask a more challenging question," Pegasus replied.

I put my hands on my hips. "And you could at least answer my question."

"It's the way of Whimsy," Pegasus said. "A door disappears each time someone closes a door. It's still a pretty good deal that the passage will be there as long as the door is opened, though. But never fear. New doors poof into existence all the time, thanks to Queen Bubbles being a great ruler."

I burst into laughter at the queen's name. And my reaction wasn't about being judgmental. A name like Queen Bubbles didn't sound like something that would inspire confidence in Whimsy citizens. Or maybe it did because everything was backwards in Whimsy. Although I wouldn't have been happy to know my ruler had a silly name.

"Anything else you want to know?" Pegasus asked.

"I'm surprised you're being polite," I said.

"I have a few minutes to spare before my next conference. It was supposed to be on the tenth of never, but the day never happened." Pegasus lowered his head down on the ground and picked something up with his beak. He devoured the item quickly.

I snorted. Whimsy once again topped itself with how ridiculous it could get. Only someone without a brain would have been oblivious to why something on the tenth of never didn't happen. Yet the peacock acted as if the conference's cancellation was breaking news.

Please. As if. Perhaps Pegasus wasn't as smart as he thought.

"Why are the leaves on the tree blue but the leaves on the ground are orange, yellow, and red?" I asked.

"That's an easy one, which makes me further question if you have any imagination. But isn't my place to judge, and I'll answer your question." Pegasus paused for a moment. "The leaves fall from the tree every couple of weeks and they turn red, orange, or yellow because trees shed their dead leaves. Although the color of its death depends on the pigment inside the leaf."

I lifted my eyebrows. "Color of its death?"

"It's a new expression I invented," Pegasus said. "Just go with it."

Okay. If the blasted peacock wanted to spout absurdisms, then that was his business. I knew better now, though, since I wouldn't let myself get lost in the confusion this time.

"Tell me the history of Whimsy, and why Flimsy and Whimsy don't speak to each other," I said.

Pegasus moved his head back and forth. "I don't think you're ready for that yet. You haven't sweated enough yet."

"What are you talking about?" I asked.

"Think about it, and all will make sense." A cloud of fog appeared after a popping sound made me cover my ears. The mist masked Pegasus, and he was gone once it disappeared.

Enzo stared me down, refusing to look elsewhere. "I'm proud of you. I hope you know that."

"And why is that?"

"Because you asked an important question."

"Do you know the history of Whimsy and Flimsy?" I asked.

Enzo smirked. "No, I don't. You didn't think you were the only one to doze off in history class, did you?"

He exhaled a deep breath. "What were you going to tell me before the sirens appeared?"

"Excuse me?"

"Don't be coy with me, Alex. You started your ramble by mentioning how something confused you."

Rain pattered against the ground while I remained silent.

Wow. I couldn't believe it. Enzo remembered I was about to tell him something important. Perhaps I underestimated him. He really was more than the kid who fell asleep in class. The only question was whether I wanted to say something and risk ruining our friendship.

But life wasn't all gloom and doom. There wasn't any chill in the air right now, despite how the rain hadn't stopped.

"I'm waiting," Enzo said.

I ran my fingers through my hair, almost wanting to scoff at its greasy texture. I couldn't even remember the last time I washed my hair.

Wait. I actually did remember the last time I washed my hair. A little less than half a day ago.

Ficklewamper. One would have thought time would go by fast. But no. It inched by slower than an old lady crossing the street. It still hadn't even been a full day since Ramona tried to poison me. Although that was only an issue of semantics, since I needed to put as much distance between Ramona and as I could.

"Maybe you should conjure a tent. We wouldn't want to get wet," I said.

Enzo grinned. "Nice try. I want to know what you were going to tell me."

"As do I," called out a voice.

Great. Pegasus returned. As if the moment couldn't get more awkward.

"I thought you had a conference to go to?" I asked.

The blasted peacock sighed. "It got canceled again. I must have gotten the date mixed up. Whatever. No good done."

I tugged at the sides of my jacket. "I think you mean no harm done."

"No." Pegasus shook his head. "I meant no good done. Gosh, I wish you would stop being so presumptuous. It's not polite."

Please. The peacock didn't just give me a lecture about being polite. That would be like a cake addict telling someone how eating desserts was dangerous.

Being addicted to eating cake wasn't funny, though. Father once told me about his cousin, who exploded into a million pieces after eating too much cake in a short period of time. And his aunt and uncle were unable to put her back together again. But that was a story for another day. I had enough problems to deal with without being worried about how people might have been oblivious to cake's danger.

My gaze narrowed. "What exactly do you at these conferences?"

"Conference?" Pegasus asked. "Did I use that word? More like party. We sit around drinking blue fizz, which is something children should never drink. It's an adult beverage. But I'm more interested to know what you want to tell your friend. Or perhaps you could tell me about your latest trial and tribulation. I could always use more material for my novel."

Please. There was no way Pegasus could have been working on a novel. And it had nothing to do with him being a peacock. He just didn't seem like the type of being who had the patience to sit down and write a novel. Doing so required a lot of focus. I, of all people, should have known that because my short stories never got anywhere. I usually wrote one line and then tossed the paper into the garbage. Father used to say I needed to stop worrying about being perfect and just write what I wanted to write and worry about editing and revising later. Although it was a shame, Father wasn't around to give me any encouragement.

"Two sirens tried to suck our souls, but they melted," I said before Enzo got the chance to pester me about what I wanted to tell him.

Pegasus beamed. "Interesting. And I suspect the reason why they melted has something to do with what you want to tell your friend."

I glared at Pegasus while the rain continued pounding onto the ground. "What are you talking about?"

"Don't play dumb. You know what I'm talking about," Pegasus said.

Enzo's jaw twitched. "Did you want to tell me that you like me as more than a friend, Alex?"

"Don't be ridiculous." A lump lingered in my throat. "I wanted to tell you how I appreciate your loyalty and helping me with my quest. That's all."

"Oh, please," Pegasus touted. "You don't think your friend is dumb enough to buy that lie, do you?"

Ficklewamper. I told another lie without realizing it.

Lying usually didn't come easy to me, though. I just didn't have a choice. It wasn't like I could blurt out my crush with Pegasus strutting around right next to us. Revealing my true feelings was something I'd tell Enzo in private.

"Enzo? Alex?" Hanna called out. "I know you're here. Just come out and make this less difficult. I promise I won't be mad."

Darn. So much for thinking Enzo and I could avoid Hanna. We couldn't. I, of all people, knew how life was more than a little complicated. I was the one who was almost poisoned by my stepmother.

"There's no door around here for me to push you through, so you might as well face the music," Pegasus said.

I scowled at Pegasus. "You better not say a word. I'm warning you. I'll shoot fire at you."

"Oh, please," Pegasus chirped. "Like you know how to use magic in Whimsy. They're over here."

A fog appeared, and he disappeared into it as footsteps shuffled against the leaves.

Ficklewamper. Pegasus just had to rat Enzo and me out.

Hanna's arrival meant being distracted about my crush, though. And that was a good thing. I was in no mood to have flushed cheeks while trying to avert my gaze. Then again, I wasn't in the mood to deal with a confrontation either.

Whatever. Hanna now stood in front of us, which meant no more time for internal rambling. At least for right now.

Enzo and I exchanged a stolen glance before looking down at the piles of leaves below us.

"I'm not here to yell," Hanna said. "I want to understand what's going on."

Enzo wrinkled his nose. "That's big of you."

I lifted my gaze off the leaves and towards Hanna. "How did you find us?"

"I used a locator spell," Hanna said.

I gasped. "Oh…"

My current shock couldn't be helped, even if Hanna hadn't confessed to do something bad. Using a locator spell meant she wasn't dumb. And I could only hope she wouldn't cause problems for Enzo and I.

"Do you wanna tell me what's going on?" Hanna asked.

I forced in a breath. Although there was one thing to be happy about. It was no longer raining right now. "It's complicated," I finally said.

Hanna gave me a weak smile. "Then why don't you start at the beginning? Make me understand why you two knuckleheads ran away from home and came to Whimsy."

There it was. That classic Hanna sass Enzo always complained about. Although Hanna still didn't resemble the monster that Enzo made her out to be. She hadn't gasped, scowled, or flinched at us. In fact, her smile even expanded from when it first formed on her face moments earlier. But I couldn't tell Hanna the truth. Being honest about something I didn't even understand myself was more than a little difficult; it was downright impossible. Or maybe, just maybe, I was making excuses. Doing so was easier than being honest with someone I wasn't sure I could trust.

11

A HISTORY LESSON

"I'm sorry you had to go through that," Hanna said sometime later while the three of us trekked through the woods.

"Thanks," I said.

Hanna blew a lock of her hair out of the way. Although I couldn't help being surprised about how her hair wasn't in a ponytail. Her hat, long-sleeved shirt, vest, khaki pants, backpack, and boots proved she was capable of preparation. Those seemed to be the types of things one would wear when hiking.

"I would have been terrified of the multiplier bees." Hanna rubbed her nose.

"Alex and I were more than terrified," Enzo said.

Hanna snickered. "You know what I meant."

"I hope I succeed in getting the crystal," I said.

Hanna returned her attention to me. "I'm sure you will. You, of all people, seem like the type of person fit for an adventure."

I halted. "And what's that supposed to mean?"

Hanna bit her lip. "Nothing. I just meant you're a unique person. It's nothing to get upset about. In fact, I'm a little envious of you."

Enzo nudged my shoulder. "See, I wasn't the only one who thought you would go on an adventure someday."

Hanna giggled. "Perhaps we have more in common than I realized."

There it was. That small snarky part of Hanna creeping through the surface, begging to come out and play. Although I made too big of a deal out of her comment. There was a difference between making a minor jab and an intentional snide comment. At least according to me. I wasn't as evil as Ramona and would never understand her mental state.

I quirked an eyebrow. "Please tell me you have a water bottle in your backpack, Hanna?"

"I'm sorry, but I don't," Hanna replied.

Okay. Maybe she wasn't as prepared as I thought she was.

Enzo took in a breath. "You should use this as an opportunity to practice your magic."

"He's right," Hanna added.

Wow. She said another nice thing about her brother. So, yeah. Maybe Enzo fibbed about his stories. But that was fine. It wasn't like he accused her of anything terrible. He just needed someone to vent to.

I stared at my hand for the longest time until a cup of water appeared. I drank it as fast as it appeared before snapping my fingers. The cup disappeared.

Hanna twirled a strand of her hair. "Can we continue? It would be nice to cover more ground before setting up camp for the night."

"Sure," I said, nodding my head.

"Great." Hanna inched forward and started picking up the pace, making Enzo and I walk faster than usual for a couple of moments so we wouldn't lag behind her.

"Please tell me you know the history of Whimsy and Flimsy, Hanna," I said. "Unless Enzo and I weren't the only ones not paying attention in history class."

Hanna grinned. "Sure. I'd be happy to. But don't beat yourselves up about not paying attention. Everyone has a loathsome class at least once in their life. The only reason I even paid attention was because my history teacher was nice."

I unzipped my jacket while sweat stuck to my face. A humid feeling spread throughout my body, yet I couldn't be shocked. Pegasus mentioned the weather changed on a moment's notice in Whimsy. Although the thought of people not being perplexed by constantly changing weather was also enough to make my head explode.

"Great," I said.

"Why don't you just take the jacket off, Alex? We both know you'll work up a sweat. But don't worry; I'll hold it." Enzo took his jacket back after I took it off and handed it to him.

Hanna coughed into her right arm. "There isn't much to say about the history. Flimsy and Whimsy used to be one country called Imsy several centuries ago."

Wow. People learn new things everyday even when not in school because I would have never guessed what Hanna just said. Not in a million years.

"However, Imsy was divided into two territories," Hanna continued. "King Justin was the last ruler to reside over Imsy while his daughter Princess Lucile ruled over Flimsy. His other daughter, Princess Katherine, ruled over Whimsy. Lucile and Katherine were still subjected to their father's authority since he was the head ruler. Although I'm guessing most people wouldn't turn up their nose at some responsibility."

Wow. She listened in class. But I was still in real danger of rambling because there had to be more to the story.

I chuckled. "Please tell me the story gets more exciting?"

"It does," Hanna said. "A growing division happened a few years into Lucile and Katherine's rule. A side note, there was only a couple of years difference between them, but they started ruling at the same time."

Enzo glared at his sister.

Hanna shook her head. "Relax. I'm getting to the important part. Anyway, the division was over magic. Flimsy believed in having order with things such as wands and requiring all citizens to have to pass a magical test and get a license when turning seventeen, while Whimsy was the exact opposite. People believed in investigating Psychochesis, which is the magic that's still around today in Whimsy. It emphasizes wish fulfillment and concentration. But people in Flimsy were afraid of it."

I scratched the back of my neck. "Interesting."

"History took a dark turn one evening when King Justin was having dinner with his Princess Lucile and Princess Katherine," Hanna said.

"What do you mean?" I asked.

"The fighting was so bad between Katherine and Lucile that it almost came to a battle. King Justin ripped his own heart out and crushed it rather than watch his daughters fight a moment longer." Hanna stared at her hand, and a cup of water appeared.

Enzo grimaced. "That's awful."

Yup. Enzo was right, no matter how obvious he sounded. I would have even thought that King Jordon was related to Ramona. Ripping out a heart seemed like the demented type of thing Ramona would have done. Then again, Ramona was too selfish to rip out her heart. And no. I wasn't making another assumption. Being obsessed with my rubies meant she was greedy and would have been less likely to injure herself.

"Lucile and Katherine agreed to a truce so they wouldn't dishonor their father's memory, and from that evening and on, Imsy was no more." Hanna finished her water before making the cup disappear.

My stomach coiled. "It's terrible it came to estrangement and their father's death."

Hanna shrugged. "That's life. Bad things happen whether we want them to or not."

Enzo chuckled. "It makes our problems seem miniscule. Wouldn't you agree, sis?"

"Anyway, that's as much as I know," Hanna said. "But I'm sure there are a ton of books written on the subject matter. I might even have some back home if you're interested."

Interesting. Hanna bypassed Enzo's comment and continued as if he hadn't said anything important.

Although doing so might have been for the best. Breaking up a brother-sister fight wouldn't have been fun.

"I wonder if things will ever change between Flimsy and Whimsy?" Enzo asked.

I snorted as we came to a clearing in the woods. "It's not like the two countries are at war or anything."

"For now, at least," Hanna said.

Hmmm. Maybe Hanna and I had more in common than I realized. Using the phrase, "for now, at least" was something I would have done. I was the world class rambler and knew all the ling for going off on tangents.

12

THE GINGERBREAD HOUSE

A gingerbread house about the size of Enzo and me put together stood before us sometime later with what I assumed to be white frosting designed into a shape of two windows and a door on the front of the house. The roof was covered in gumdrops, which was outlined in more white frosting.

I sighed. "Thank goodness. I'm starving. I'm sure nobody will mind if I help myself to a few gumdrops."

I rushed over to the house. There was a reason for the grumblings in my stomach because I hadn't eaten anything since breakfast today.

"Look at the sign, Alex!" Hanna screamed.

Concentrating on floating allowed me to leap into the air for a few moments and grab a few gumdrops. Something honked, and I fell to the ground, which was covered in snow. Not frosting. I could tell the difference.

Frosting was sticky whereas snow was cold and odorless, which was what the white stuff was.

Gumdrops soon fell onto the ground. I then shifted my gaze back towards the house. I almost recoiled at the two signs with poles from the bottom of the sign to the ground, which somehow escaped my attention. The first sign said: **EATING ANY CANDY ON THE GINGERBREAD HOUSE COULD RESULT IN ARREST AND LOSING YOUR HEAD.** The other sign said: **WARNING! EATING ANY FOOD FROM THE HOUSE, WILL SOUND THE ALARM AND CAUSE FLAMINGOS TO APPEAR**.

"Are you okay, Alex?" Enzo offered me his hand, and I took it.

I remained silent. This was one of the few times when I didn't have anything to say.

Hanna rubbed the back of her neck. "I wish you hadn't grabbed the gumdrops."

"This is the stupidest thing I've heard of in Whimsy, and I've heard a lot." I drew in a deep breath. "Why have a giant edible house just for looks?"

"Because it's Whimsy," Enzo blurted.

I clenched my jaw. "Good point."

Agreeing with Enzo was necessary no matter how stupid or absurd the edible house seemed. He had a point. Nothing ever made sense in Whimsy.

The whimsical nature of the country was comforting in a strange way, though. There was something relieving about having freedom and looser boundaries. At least in my mind. Because I was still a kid.

The cawing sounds grew louder, making us crane our heads, only to realize dozens of flamingos were now in front of us.

"Ficklewamper!" Hanna curled her fingers into a fist.

Okay. Good to know I wasn't the only who used extreme words sometimes. Now also was as good of time as any to use the word, "ficklewamper."

My jaw trembled. "What do we do?"

Hanna hissed. "Let's see what they want."

The flamingo with a gold crown on his head marched over to us. "I'm King Fabio of the flamingos, and one of you has just made a big mistake. Which one of you tried to eat and/or succeeded with eating something from the gingerbread house?"

"I did," I murmured.

Honesty was one thing. Enjoying it was another, though. I could only imagine what would happen to me. Doing the right thing was still important, since I couldn't let Hanna and Enzo get in trouble for something I did. I might have been a lot of things, but I refused to be a coward. Nope. Not ever. Being a coward meant I would have been similar to Ramona. And that could never happen. Not even if she and I were the last two people alive.

"Then we have no choice but to take you to Queen Bubbles," King Fabio said. "And you will most likely lose your head."

Hanna grunted. "But he didn't eat the gumdrops."

"It doesn't matter," King Fabio said. "The gingerbread house is a national monument."

Enzo did his usual pleading gesture and pressed his hands together. "Please, King Fabio. There must be something we can do. Couldn't you look the other way? He's an orphan."

King Fabio stomped his talons on the layer of snow covering the ground. "I'm sorry, but rules are rules. No exceptions for anyone."

King Fabio lowered his head, opening his beak as he was about to grab my sleeve before Hanna shoved my forehead.

"Run, Alex!" Hanna screamed.

Enzo grabbed my hand, and darted forward before I processed what happened. I cocked my head. Another door hovered on the left side of the back of the house. My pulse soared while Enzo's shoes sloshed against the snow before I arrived at the door after another beat. Hanna was right behind us, as was King Fabio.

Enzo opened the door while we continued holding hands. We then leapt inside the doorway while I closed my eyes.

"You aren't going to get Alex if it's the last thing I do." Hanna's voice echoed. The door slammed shut, making my ears ring.

The three of us thumped against the ground. I was on top of Enzo while Hanna was lying on me.

We stood. Then I dusted myself off as I took in the scenery around me. Okay. These trees had purple leaves. Still couldn't say I was surprised, though, because Whimsy was always throwing new things at us.

Hanna played with a strand of her hair. "That was close."

I forced a laugh. "Too close."

"The important thing is we're okay," Enzo said.

I sighed. "I really am sorry for grabbing the gumdrops. It was an honest, stupid mistake, and I'll be more careful in the future."

Hanna raised her hand at me. "It's okay. Let's just have dinner and set up camp here since we have space."

Yeah. She didn't misspeak. This part of the forest wasn't drenched in trees like the other parts of Whimsy were.

13

TRUTH TIME

"Thanks for not judging me," I said hours later, while sitting on a log next to Enzo.

The fire crackled while the full moon glowed, providing extra light. The star lighting up the night sky helped too, since anything that was in the opposite column of pitch blackness was a good thing.

Snoring came from one of the two tents Hanna set up using magic echoed, making me grin.

Sure. There was nothing super funny about Hanna going to bed before Enzo and I. But one would have thought she would have fallen asleep last. She was two years older than us.

Enzo squeezed my hand. "No problem. You know I'm always here for you."

My heart skipped several beats. I just couldn't help myself, because saying things such as what Enzo just said more than messed with my head. And in a perfect world, I would have had clarity regarding my feelings about Enzo. But no. Life was anything but perfect.

I sighed. "I lied to you, Enzo."

"I know."

"You do?"

"You're my best friend, and I can always tell when you aren't being truthful."

I continued looking at the leaves in front of my feet, even though there was no reason for me to have pangs of shame wavering through my body. "I don't know how it happened," I said.

Enzo chuckled. "You can look me in the eye. I'm a big boy. I know I sometimes stared at you longer than I should have, made offhanded comments, patted your shoulder one too many times for one too many seconds, in addition to leaning closer."

"What are you saying?" I asked.

"It's not one sided."

"I thought you liked girls."

"I only said that stuff in the past to see your reaction." Enzo laughed louder.

I turned towards him. "I was just trying to be a supportive friend."

Enzo swooshed his head back and forth several times. "Maybe we need to be more open with our feelings."

I nodded. "Good idea."

Enzo winked. "How long have you known you aren't like other guys?"

I frowned, remaining silent. Sure. We might have been best friends, which meant Enzo would never intentionally hurt me. But I could have a pang of nervousness jolt my body. Enzo's remark created a sense of uneasiness because he should have taken a minute to think before speaking.

"I didn't mean anything bad by it," Enzo continued. "I just meant how long have you known you've like guys instead of girls?"

I shrugged. "I don't know. I guess I always knew."

"Yeah, me too." Enzo took another swig of his water from the cup resting on the ground next to him before it disappeared.

"And this is why you're so protective and accompanied me?" I asked.

Enzo didn't even flinch. "Yes."

"Thank you for being honest. I know that must not have been easy for you."

"Same." Enzo leaned in and gave me a quick peck on the lips.

Okay. Maybe there was more to life than worrying about the horrors from bedtime tales coming true. It was possible sometimes for people to get what they want. And I'd hold onto Enzo reciprocating my feelings for as long as I could. It was about time I had good news.

I wouldn't be blinded by having a nice moment with Enzo, though. Ramona was still out there somewhere. And there was no telling how much time I had until our inevitable confrontation.

14

THE KRAKEN SHOWDOWN

Enzo and I stood outside of our tent the following morning while a few clouds stained the otherwise pale blue sky as birds zipped by. Hanna was still asleep, and Enzo and I had yet to make breakfast and a table appear.

"We need to talk," Enzo said.

I picked at my nail. "We don't have to talk about last night if you don't want to."

Enzo grabbed my hand. "But I do."

"Okay..."

"It was nice. It felt right."

A part of me wanted to smile. Most people might not have been lucky enough to have their crush reciprocate. But I wasn't most people. Enzo was the one who gave me the quick kiss. Not the other way around. In fact, I still wanted to pinch myself no matter how childish the idea seemed, because the whole thing couldn't be real. The problem was I had been used to misery for so long as a result of Mother's death and then Father's death that it now seemed like the only thing I deserved.

My eyebrows inched up. "You don't regret the kiss?"

"Not for a second, and please don't be shocked."

"I can't help it."

"I know, I know. And I have to admit it's partly why you're charming."

I winked at him. Doing so was nice because he was the one who always did that to me. "You find me charming?"

Enzo's cheeks reddened. "You don't have to make a big deal about it, Alex."

I laughed. "I was only joking. Lighten up."

"I'm usually the one who has to tell you that."

I coughed into my arm. "There's something I wanted to ask you before Hanna wakes up."

Enzo leaned forward a little. "And what's that?"

"Hanna's been pretty nice. You don't think she's up to something, do you?"

Yup. I once again had to consider the various possibilities of a situation.

Sure. I wanted to believe Hanna meant well. But skepticism was natural after living with Stepmother Dreariest.

"And what's that supposed to mean?" Enzo asked.

I hung my head lower. "I didn't mean anything bad by it. I just meant Hanna doesn't seem like the same Hanna you've described to me numerous times."

Enzo hesitated. "Yeah. I hate to do admit it, but the same thought crossed my mind."

Good to know we had similar thoughts. I mean, sure. We didn't need to have everything in common. But it was nice to know we were compatible-even if in a small way.

I gave him an inquisitive look. "Then what should we do?"

Enzo locked his fingers together. "Let's keep an eye on the situation for now. It's not like we saw her do anything bad."

"Fair enough."

Yeah, I meant what I said. Enzo could have defended his sister out of loyalty. But no. He valued my feelings by not delegitimizing them.

Something thumped against the leaves, making us turn our heads.

Saying I was surprised at the person who just fell onto the ground would have been the understatement of the century. There was no way I ever expected to run into Francis again. Yet I had.

"What's going on?" I asked.

Francis got up from the ground without even brushing the dust off himself. Although doing so wasn't important. The thick layer of morning dew coating the ground would have irritated me if I were him. Getting even a little wet would have been a pain since I still wasn't comfortable with how magic worked in Whimsy. But that was me. I was a visitor from Flimsy. And if Whimsy citizens were fine with magic being spontaneous, then that was their business.

Francis took in a deep breath while something pounded against the ground and grew louder with each passing second. "You need to run!"

I crossed my arms. "You're going to have to be more specific."

"Alex is right," Enzo said.

The gesture might have been minor. Knowing Enzo still had my back and once again agreed with me was nice, though.

Francis gripped his chest with his hand while continuing to catch his breath. "See for yourself. But don't say I didn't warn you."

"You still didn't answer my question." I continued glaring at Francis.

Ficklewamper. Francis seemed like a nice guy despite his past as a pirate. Yet he just did the same thing Pegasus did.

Being evasive was no way to win points with me. Some people needed to learn the importance of not wasting time. Although I wasn't one to talk. Someone could accuse me of not always being direct.

Whatever. I was a work in progress and had no shame without being the epitome of perfection. After all, I was only twelve years old.

Something pounded against the ground, making me scream as soon as I stared above. Carlyle the Kraken towered over the three of us. And it didn't even matter if I pinched myself several times because the monster was still there after each time.

"I thought krakens only lived in the water?" I asked.

"Nope!" Francis yelled. "They also live on land in Whimsy."

I might not have known a lot about magic in Whimsy. But I could try to help. Doing so was the least I could for Francis, since he helped Enzo and I out yesterday.

The image of a spark formed in my mind while I raised my palms. The ember multiplied and grew in volume while remaining etched in my brain until turning into a full-blown sea of red, orange, and yellow. Flames spat out of both my hands while Carlyle almost grabbed Francis with one of its numerous tentacles. The kraken screamed several times before moving backward. But it didn't matter how times the kraken acted out because my mind remained focused on the image of the fire. The flames shot up the tentacle and onto the left side of the Kraken's face before sparks flew off in numerous directions and traveled down the rest of the tentacles. And it was only a matter of seconds before the kraken was engulfed in fire. The fire disappeared after another beat, leaving only ashes behind. Almost as if the flames swallowed the kraken. A gust of wind soon blew the ashes in the opposite direction.

Francis grinned. "You defeated Carlyle."

"I hope you aren't mad at me … I know it was your vendetta," I said.

Francis raised his hand. "Please. I'm not that stubborn."

I chuckled. "Good to know. Although I have one question."

"You can ask me anything," Francis said.

"Why didn't you use magic to defeat the kraken?" I asked.

Francis averted his gaze. "I'm not very good at magic."

"Well, I'm glad I could help," I said.

Francis's eyes lit up. "You shouldn't be glad. You should be proud of yourself. It's not every day a mere boy defeats a monster."

"I don't think I'm special or anything," I said.

Francis shook his head. "That's not my point. I just meant you did a great thing. Anyway, I should go. I have a very invigorating conference to go to."

I stole a glance at Enzo. We both burst into laughter before we could control ourselves. There was no way my thought could be true. Yet we were in Whimsy, and plenty of strange things had already happened.

"What's so funny?" Francis asked.

I bit my lip. "You wouldn't happen to know a peacock by the name of Pegasus, would you?"

"Yes, I do. Why do you ask?" Francis rubbed his hook, which accentuated the gold's shininess.

"It's a long story," I said.

Francis's eyebrows swung up. "Do you want me to give him a message?"

"No," Enzo said. "I think I can speak for Alex when I say it's good when we don't hear from Pegasus."

I gave Francis a mock scowl. "Enzo's right. Although the jig is up. I know what's really going on at the so-called conference."

Francis almost choked. "Pegasus told you about the blue fizz?"

"Yes. But I can't say I'm surprised. You must know all about the blue fizz, since you're a former pirate," I said.

Francis coughed. "Yes, I do. But you two shouldn't drink blue fizz till you're older. Like in a hundred years."

Okay. Good to know Francis cared about our well-being—even if he didn't know much about any other details of our lives.

"I should get going, but I have a feeling you'll see me around. Anyway, I'll chat with Pegasus. Even I can admit he's a bit much sometimes." Francis leaped for a nearby door before jumping through it. He slammed the door behind him before it disintegrated into dust.

"Hanna's gone," Enzo said after stepping out of her tent a moment later.

I rolled my eyes. "What do you mean? I thought she was still asleep."

"I'm serious, Alex. Go see for yourself."

I kneeled, then peeked inside Hanna's tent. The wind rattled in the background as a few leaves fell from the trees as they turned into red, orange, and yellow.

Ficklewamper.

Enzo was right. Hanna was gone, and my heart once again fluttered in my chest.

So, yeah. I hoped everything would be okay despite how I didn't have a crystal ball and couldn't look into the future. Because I needed to be honest with myself. I had a strange feeling that something bad was gonna happen. Like when someone's joints ached when there was a change in barometric pressure.

15

RAMONA'S BACK

"What should we do?" I asked while we continued standing outside of Hanna's tent. A dull shade of gray clouds replaced the previous sunny sky while rain fell onto the ground. Although there was no reason to get upset. It was only a drizzle as opposed to a massive storm. Intense rain storms were nothing to laugh about, though. Father once told me a story about one of his friends who got lost in a rain storm never to been seen again. But that was a story for another day. I didn't have time to think about something morbid because Hanna's absence was troublesome enough.

Enzo shrugged. "I don't know. I mean, yeah. I'm concerned. But I don't want to invent a problem until we know something is wrong."

"I would suggest that we eat breakfast, but it is drizzling," I said.

"We could eat inside the tent."

"Going in the tent is a good idea, but I'm not hungry. Don't let me stop you if you're starving, though."

I followed Enzo back into the tent as he zipped it up. We then sat down on our respective sleeping bags.

Going back into the tent was a good idea because the rain started slamming into the ground, almost like Father's rain story that I thought about moments earlier.

Enzo grinned. "I want you to know I'm proud of you. Defeating the kraken took guts."

"I was just experimenting with magic. It wasn't like I'm some skilled genius. It could be a fluke."

"Why do you always sell yourself short, Alex? You're a great guy and have a lot of admirable qualities. Never forget that."

Okay. I wouldn't stop Enzo from praising me if he wanted to. But I didn't expect him to worship the ground I walked on. And I wasn't even trying to be modest. I would never admit the truth. Yet there had been more than a few nervous pangs rolling through my body when I stared Carlyle the Kraken right in the eye.

Check that. It was more like I stared death in the face. But it didn't matter what I called the kraken. It was still a monster, regardless of what label I used.

"Can I tell you a secret?" I asked.

"Sure. But you know better than to ask. I want to know whatever you feel comfortable telling me."

"Sometimes I wish I could bring my parents back from the dead." I wiped my eyes before Enzo could notice my tears.

Yeah. There was no shame in showing emotion. But I couldn't help myself. It was bad enough that I would have won the award for rambler of the year—if such an award existed, that was. However, I didn't want to be viewed as unstable. Sure. Emotional distress was a part of life. Especially when dealing with the loss of two parents so early in life. It didn't matter who the person was. Saying I lost both of my parents at a young age would never roll off my tongue. At least not without shuddering a little.

Enzo got up from his sleeping bag. Then he walked over to mine before sitting down and grabbing my hand.

"I'll tell you a secret since you told me one," Enzo said.

"I'm listening."

"I miss my parents, too."

Phew. As if I ever needed to worry about my dynamic with Enzo. There was always a natural give and take. Being with him didn't take much effort. He also told me personal things as this moment proved. But now wasn't the time to bring up Father's childhood friend, who he couldn't name ten facts about.

"How do you live with the pain?" An uneasy feeling jabbed my stomach. Or maybe it was hunger. I could never be sure about anything these days. Except that I liked Enzo as more than a friend.

Enzo sighed. "It takes time."

"The worst part is I feel stupid."

"And why's that?"

"I believed Ramona cared about me." I sobbed into his shoulder.

Enzo rubbed my hand. "It's never wrong to give someone the benefit of the doubt. It's normal."

"And now your sister has run off to goodness knows where and has probably gotten herself into more trouble than I can even imagine."

Yeah. Caring about being dramatic was neither here nor there because it would have been nice if Hanna told us where she went. That was the polite thing to do. Check that. It wasn't the polite thing to do. It was the only thing to do. It would have been different if we were only three kids camping. But we weren't. I was trying to defeat Ramona, which qualified as an unusual situation.

He sighed. "Maybe not."

I lifted my head off Enzo's shoulder. "Can I ask you another question?"

"You didn't just say that."

"I'm sorry."

"Stop apologizing," he said.

I bit my lip. "What do you see in me?"

"You're a genuine great person," he said.

We just continued looking each other in the eye while I wished this moment could last forever. Sure. My thought might have been corny. But I couldn't help myself. Having a minute of calmness was necessary as a result of the chaos that happened since Ramona tried to kill me.

A voice cackled from outside the tent, making my back hairs rise. "I'm not so sure about that."

I smacked my hand over my mouth while exchanging a glance with Enzo. He then grabbed my free hand.

"You should come out of the tent because I know you're in there," Ramona said.

Wow. The return of my wicked stepmother was what I needed to jump for joy and be the happiest kid in both Flimsy and Whimsy. NOT. I was nowhere near ready to deal with Ramona. Not ever. At least until I retrieved the crystal from the Kuku mountains and hatched a plan with Marino the Great.

"Alex, Enzo!!" Ramona spat. "This is my final warning. If you don't step out in the next ten seconds, then I'll rip Hanna's heart right from out of her chest and kill her. Or if that won't work, perhaps I'll just set the tent on fire, and you can burn to death."

16

HANNA'S BETRAYAL

Ficklewamper. Ficklewamper. Ficklewamper. Enzo and I had no choice but to exit the tent. Having Hanna die or burn to death were both terrible options, since there was no positive spin on them.

I gasped the second I stood outside of the tent. Hanna stood next to Ramona with her hands tied behind her back.

"How did you find me?" I asked.

"I'm so sorry," Hanna whined.

Ramona clutched her pearl necklace. "It really is an interesting story. Do you want to tell them, or should I, Hanna?"

Hmmm. Perhaps my stomach's lurching had just cause, even if I hadn't any concrete facts at the time. Intuition existed for a reason, and I should have trusted how something might have been off with Hanna. But now wasn't the time to pass judgment. I needed to get the facts. Although I was pretty sure that everyone in Whimsy had no issue with passing judgment before examining a situation's facts. It was the just type of country that Whimsy was.

Enzo frowned. "What is she talking about, Hanna?"

Ramona nudged Hanna's shoulder. "Don't be bashful, dear. You should be proud of yourself. You even you remind me a little bit of myself when I was your age."

"I didn't mean to betray you guys," Hanna said.

I stomped my feet. "You still haven't answered my question, you vipleviper."

Ramona smirked. "We really should enlighten them. Keeping people in suspense is rude."

A tear rolled down Hanna's cheek while tree branches bobbed in the wind as more rain fell from the sky. "You have to understand how desperate I was for the money. I was doing it for us, Enzo," Hanna said.

"I went over to Hanna's house shortly after I recovered from the nasty river spell trick you pulled on me and made her a deal. If she helped me track you down, then I would give her twenty percent of the rubies. And lucky for her, Enzo was also missing, so she had a stake in the game." Ramona's smile expanded.

I screamed at Hanna. "How could you do this to me? I'm your brother's best friend."

"I think we're more than best friends," Enzo interrupted.

Ouch. I should have known better than to label Enzo as a friend after we kissed and talked about our feelings. It was a safe bet that I would have had a cow if I were in Enzo's position because I wouldn't want my boyfriend to only introduce me as a friend. Whatever. My mistake had nothing to do with being callous or careless. It was a minor slip of tongue because I felt no shame at being attracted to Enzo. The worrier inside me meant I couldn't help myself, though. I hadn't realized Enzo was ready to go public about us.

Ramona's nostrils flared. "Nobody cares about your bisexual melodrama."

My jaw lowered. "You know I'm bisexual?"

"Yup." Ramona laughed.

Hanna glanced at Enzo. "I didn't realize you liked guys."

Enzo crossed his arms. "I don't owe you any explanations."

Hanna clenched her jaw. "You misunderstood me. I'm not mad or anything; I'm just surprised."

"I trusted you, Hanna," I said.

"I couldn't go through with it," Hanna blurted.

I glanced at my stepmother, who nodded.

"It's unfortunately true," Ramona said. "I began to get suspicious of Hanna, so I used magic to track her down before forcing her out of the tent last night and into my clutches,"

Hanna gritted her teeth. "I really switched sides. You have to believe me."

"It doesn't matter now, dear." Ramona rubbed her hair, which was wrapped in a bun.

I scoffed at my stepmother as snow fell to the ground as opposed to rain. Figures. The weather would always be unpredictable, and to expect anything else would have been foolish.

"What do you want?" I asked.

Ramona cackled even louder this time. "Isn't it obvious? I want to finish my mission, which was why I have a new bargain for you, Alex."

I put my hands on my hips. "And what's that?

"I won't harm one hair of Hanna's or Enzo's if you come with me willingly," Ramona said.

I furrowed an eyebrow. "I have no reason to trust you."

"You might not like me, but my main goal is the rubies, not harming Hanna and Enzo. Only one person has to die." Ramona pursed her lips.

Enzo tilted his head. "Don't do it, Alex—not after everything that's been said between us. You mean too much to me."

Ramona snorted. "How sad for you two. Being a better person would mean pretending to give a ficklewamper about your budding relationship. But I'm not a good person because I could care less."

Wow. Ramona admitted she was evil. But it wasn't like I would give her a medal. Having self-awareness didn't make her a good person. It just meant she wasn't stupid. And that wasn't exactly something to jump for joy about. Because I didn't care if Ramona saved my life. I would never forgive her for almost poisoning me because of greed.

"I still don't get why you're obsessed with those darn rubies," I said.

A vein surfaced on Ramona's head. "Haven't you been paying attention? Nobody loved your father as much I did. You're just a kid."

Okay. Good to know how she really felt.

"I've had enough of your babbling." Hanna jerked her arms, which sent the rope falling to the snow-blanketed ground, as I shuddered after cold air nipped my face.

"I hope you like quicksand," Hanna raised her palms as a tan colored substance formed both beneath and behind my stepmother.

Ramona shot through the quicksand and was out of sight.

Hanna pressed her hands together and a bunch of vines with prickers spat out from the quicksand laced ground and stopped after inching a few feet in the air.

"That should hold her," she said.

"Will she suffocate?" I asked.

Yup. Trying to be a good person meant worrying about killing Ramona. Sure. She was my least favorite person. Although I didn't believe in resorting to violence. And no. I wasn't being too nice. I just didn't like the idea of using violence to solve my problems. Unless someone threatened my life. But now wasn't the time to postulate about anything. Enzo and I still had to deal with Hanna's betrayal.

"No," Hanna said. "Quicksand doesn't do that. It will just trap her because magic doesn't work in quick sand. Plus, the vines reach to where she is," Hanna said.

"Come on, Alex. We're leaving." Enzo grabbed my hand and dragged me to a door a few feet behind us.

Hanna whimpered. "Where are you going?"

Enzo glanced back at Hanna for a beat. "You can't be trusted. So, please don't follow us."

Enzo opened the door and slammed it shut before we leapt onto the next leg of our adventure.

Free falling wasn't fun. But at least Ramona was dealt with. For the moment, that was. Even I knew she'd return again someday.

17

A NEW IDEA

Enzo and I thumped against the ground. He got up first and offered his hand before I took in the scenery. Various items were on display-some in glass cages and others hanging on the wall. An **OPEN** sign faced the inside of the store, which meant that the **CLOSED** side of the sign must have been on display outside.

"Where are we?" Enzo asked.

"I think it might be a pawn shop."

Laughing at Enzo would have been appropriate in any other situation. But not now. He chose me over his sister moments earlier. And it wasn't like I wanted him to regret his choice. Because that was the last thing I wanted or needed. We had only recently admitted we both liked each other as more than friends.

Wanting to start things off with as little drama as possible also wasn't a complicated idea. It was bad enough that we had the drama going on with Ramona and

Hanna's betrayal. So, a cynical person would have even gone as far as to say that circumstances weren't on our side.

I snickered.

Whatever. Enzo and I only suffered a little drama. It wasn't the end of the world because the situation could be much worse despite the sweat trickling out of my pores right now.

"What the blazes is going on?" croaked a voice.

A man with tied back hair, a tunic, khaki pants, and a peg leg shuffled from a room in the back of the store. I wasn't going to lie, though. Not now. Sure. Judging someone by his or her appearance might have been unfair. But it was only natural. And it wasn't even because the man had one wooden leg. Nope. That wasn't the case. His two scars above his eyes were what made fear vibrate through my body.

He put his hands on his hips. "Don't you two boys know how to read? The sign says we're closed."

My attention drifted back to the door, and I shook my head. Wow. I was so lost in my own thoughts that I didn't even realize frost coated the windows and door. Figures. The weather just had to be on the cold side.

I coughed. "We fell through a door. We were trying to get away from someone."

His lips quivered. "I've gone through many doors too."

"We didn't mean any harm," I said.

Enzo's gaze lowered to the man's wooden leg. I elbowed him before leaning into his ear. "It's rude to stare," I whispered.

Enzo sighed. "I can't help it."

The man snickered. "Looking at my leg, are you?"

"He didn't mean any offense," I said before Enzo could say something that might get us in more trouble.

Speaking for Enzo might have been rude, but it was the only thing I could do. Sure. Enzo wasn't a mean person. However, I couldn't risk him saying the wrong thing. Surviving the two kraken encounters, the sirens, Pegasus the peacock's antics, and Ramona's comeback was miracle enough.

The man didn't flinch. "It's okay. Talking about the accident helps."

My eyebrows knitted together. "Accident?"

"Yeah," said the man. "I stepped into a volcano with the leg that's now wooden. Anyway, the name's Smith."

Enzo's eyes bulged up. "How are you still alive? Wouldn't you have died from the burns?'

"Volcanos are different in Whimsy," I said. "They look like fire, but they don't burn people. They just vaporize whatever falls into it."

Enzo folded his arms. "And how do you know that?"

"I paid attention to Hanna when she revealed that tidbit." Another gaze around the shop made me chuckle again, despite how nothing funny happened. Father always used to tell me that I needed to be more organized and shouldn't have hoarded so much stuff. Yet here I was. Standing in a shop filled with people's things that they no longer wanted. It was actually kind of ironic.

"I'll never forgive Francis," Smith said, shaking his head.

My eyes lit up. "You wouldn't by chance happen to be talking about Francis the pirate, would you?"

"Why?" Smith asked. "Do you know him?"

I took in a deep breath. "Yeah. I do. Anyway, why do you blame Francis?"

"Because we were outrunning that blasted kraken. And it didn't help that Pegasus was there too." Smith sipped his tea, which I forgot to mention was on the glass counter behind him. Although it was good that he hadn't sipped it as soon as he saw it. Steam seeped out of the cup when I first noticed the shop's surroundings.

Enzo ran his fingers through his hair, probably trying to give himself a distraction. And a part of me was relieved by that possibility. Good to know I might not have been the only one who was nervous.

"Sounds like you've had an interesting life," Enzo said.

"That isn't even the worst part." Smith paused. "Francis's wife was my wife first."

"Yet you still remained friends?" Another glance around the shop made me fixate on a gold watch a few feet away from me.

Ficklewamper. How I would have given anything to own something fancy even if Father had been well off. I just couldn't put my finger on it because there was something intoxicating from the shining gold.

"It's complicated," Smith said.

Enzo grabbed my hand before forcing a smile at Smith. "Alex and I should leave."

Smith rolled his eyes. "Nonsense. You just got here. Besides, I don't even remember the last time I had a customer."

"You're closed right now," I added.

Smith grabbed a cookie from his pocket. I could only imagine the explosion of the butter and sugar flavors jolting his taste buds. But it wasn't like I had a cookie that long ago, since Ramona's failed poisoning was the last time that I enjoyed one. Smith continued making crunching sounds for a few more seconds while it took all the control I had not to drool.

Smith shrugged. "Closed. Open. Who can tell?"

Smith's comment was enough to make my mind race. It was another example of Whimsy's logical fallacies.

"There's one thing you could help us with," I said.

Smith gripped his medallion. "And what's that?"

"Do you have anything that blocks locator spells?" I asked. "Enzo and I are trying to avoid someone."

"Sure. Give me one moment." Smith scurried to one of the glass enclosures before taking out his key and opening the display case closest to him. He took out two rings and gave one to both Enzo and me.

Enzo looked the ring over. It was an emerald. "But we don't have any money."

"I can make an exception. Just return them when you no longer need them," Smith said.

I smiled. "Thanks. It's really kind of you to go out on a limb for us. Anyway, would you mind answering one more question?"

Smith nodded. "Sure. Go ahead."

"Where are we in Whimsy? Enzo and I are a little lost," I said.

"You're in the capital city of Dimsy." Smith took out the ribbon from his hair, letting his hair free, which fell several inches past his shoulders.

"Are we near to the Kuku mountains?" I asked.

"Nope. You're only about halfway there," Smith said.

"Thanks. Anyway, have a good day." I shuffled towards the entrance, and Enzo followed after me.

The man squealed. "You have a good day, young sirs. You don't know how happy you've made me by giving me company."

Couldn't say I was surprised by another nonsensical thing—I wasn't. Even if it wasn't a law or a creature. I was still in Whimsy and it would have been foolish to expect anything less. There were also worse places to be than Whimsy because any second without Ramona was a good second.

The placard containing a dragon image clinked when the door opened. The door lingered for a second after Enzo stepped onto the sidewalk behind me.

"That was fun. Let's do it again sometime," I said.

Enzo grimaced. "Let's not."

Hmmm. Perhaps Whimsy caused more stress for Enzo than he realized.

Whatever. I knew better than to push Enzo to discuss something. He would have mentioned his stress if he wanted to. And no. Not giving him an opening to discuss his stress didn't make me a bad friend. It wasn't like I would shut him up if I he brought up the topic. I just had a lot to contemplate. We couldn't avoid Hanna and

Ramona forever, no matter how nice doing so might have been.

The wind rattled, pushing a piece of paper towards us. I leaned on the ground, but Enzo snatched the poster before I could."

"Wait!" Enzo exclaimed. "This could be fun. And it's at noon, which is coming faster than you think."

Enzo continued holding onto the paper. Almost as if his life depended on gripping it as tight as possible.

I pointed to the bottom of the poster. "Check the fine print. The royal masked ball is by invitation only."

Enzo snorted. "I don't care. It's about time we had some fun."

Okay. Maybe Enzo was more of a rebel than I realized if he wanted to crash the ball. And that fact kinda excited me. Maybe it was time to live life a little on edge. I could try to enjoy myself for a moment or two, after all. Because I'd probably resume worrying sooner rather than later.

18

CLOTHES SHOPPING

"Where are we even supposed to get outfits?" I asked moments later while Enzo and I continued standing on the sidewalk.

He pointed his finger across the street. "There, silly! Now let's hurry up!"

My lips quivered. "This is a very bad idea."

Enzo raised an eyebrow. "And why's that?"

"We've already digressed enough with everything that's happened. We have to go to the Kuku mountains because Ramona won't be captive forever," I said.

Assuming Ramona would break free had nothing to do with inventing problems that didn't exist. It was the only logical explanation. Problems didn't just magically disappear. Besides, the woman might have given me more goosebumps than I cared to admit it. But I wasn't an idiot and couldn't deny how she was smart. Ramona was the one who almost succeeded with poisoning me, after all.

Enzo's gaze remained on me. "It could help us. Maybe we could find someone to help us."

I pouted. "I don't know. Do you want to risk one more thing going wrong?"

"Quit complaining, Alex. Things aren't as bad as they seem." He paused for a beat. "Sure. We've had some minor hiccups. But we've always survived."

Please. Our challenges were more than minor hiccups.

The wind howled, pushing several cans down the street. Although now wasn't the time to complain about littering.

"I'm not taking no for an answer." Enzo grabbed my hand and dragged me across the street before I could even blink.

"I still don't think this is a good idea," I said after we entered the shop a moment later.

"Enough," Enzo spat.

The door creaked. Then, I glanced inside the shop while the scent of peppermint wafted through the air. Whimsy might have been a lot of things. But I couldn't say that the stores were bad since there were aisles and aisles of clothing. Almost as if we were already at the royal castle.

A woman who was in her early thirties trekked over to us. Although I hadn't made an assumption. Her shirt said: Proud thirty-two-year-old. She also sported a long-sleeved shirt, pants, slip-on shoes, besides having luscious pink hair that came down to her waist. And no. Luscious wasn't a dramatic word. Her hair was that thick. Although the girl's eye patch was her most interesting feature. That didn't seem to be the type of thing a person witnessed every day. Commenting about her eyepatch wasn't about mocking her, though. It was only an observation because a pang of nostalgia rolled through my body. My mind couldn't help but drift back to Drake-even if there was a good chance the girl wasn't a pirate.

She tucked a strand of hair behind her ear. "Can I help you two lads with something?"

"We were wondering if you had something that might be appropriate for a masked ball?" Enzo said before I could even open my mouth.

She stroked her chin. "You were invited to the masked ball?"

"Yes," Enzo replied.

Okay. I couldn't stop Enzo from lying if he was intent on doing so. But I also didn't have to enjoy it. Being honest meant admitting dishonesty wasn't a favorable trait, even if life was more complicated than right or wrong. Then again, there was a difference between telling a small lie and being a habitual liar.

She rubbed her hands together. "How exciting. I've always wanted to get an invitation, but I've never gotten one."

I rolled my eyes. "How unfortunate."

"I see your friend is the king of sarcasm," she said to Enzo.

My stomach churned. "Talk to me, not about me."

Yup. I had no problem standing up for myself, even if every little thing didn't need to be an argument. My feelings mattered, and I refused for anyone to be condescending or demeaning towards me.

"Fair enough. I'm Evelyn." She extended her hand. Then Enzo and I both shook it.

Enzo coughed into his arm. "Do you have something for us?"

There it was again. Enzo's old self because he was getting things back on track. But he didn't deserve a medal because he got us off track in the first place.

"What's the rush?" Evelyn asked. "We just started a lovely conversation."

Ficklewamper. Slapping my hand over my head was necessary since even I was about ready to scoff at the woman. Because some people didn't have all the time in the world to waste.

"Something wrong?" Enzo whispered into my ear.

I shook my head. "Nope. I'm great."

Evelyn sighed. "My mother used to complain about feeling rushed all the time."

"What do you mean, 'used to?'" Enzo asked.

"It's a long story," she said.

"Our sizes are a child's large," Enzo said.

Thank goodness Enzo used his brain for once. Evelyn's preface was all I needed to hear, to realize we would be here all day if she had her way. Or maybe I was impatient, and should have been more accepting of others. Nope. That wasn't it. Even the most patient person would have been annoyed by Evelyn. Her job involved customer service since she worked at a clothing store. Yet she wasted our time because she still hadn't helped us yet.

Evelyn grinned. "I've got the thing."

"We'll need masks too," Enzo said.

Evelyn nodded. "Of course."

Evelyn shuffled away from us and was soon out of sight. But that was a good thing because there was no telling what would come out of her mouth next.

Enzo gave me a dirty look. "You have to lighten up, man."

Wow. Life was more chaotic than a swinging pendulum. Enzo was the one who had been stressed out when we exited the previous shop. But no. Apparently, his previous emotional state was no longer relevant to him.

"I'm sorry, but I can't do that ... We have a mission," I said.

"I know. But it's as if your whole life depends on defeating Ramona."

I gritted my teeth. "It kinda does. She already tried to kill me in case you've forgotten."

"No. I haven't forgotten."

"You have no idea how that kind of betrayal feels like."

"I might have a better idea than you think," he said.

Oops. I made a big mistake, because I should have realized Hanna's betrayal must have stung Enzo. So, yeah. I couldn't help feeling slightly guilty. In a perfect world, I would have been more mindful of Enzo's feelings. Enzo had done so much for me, and that fact required gratitude. Enzo didn't have to be supportive. Yet he was. No explanation was necessary about how some people wouldn't be as reliable as Enzo.

Evelyn's feet squeaked across the ground while she carried the outfits and two masks. She handed one outfit and mask to each of us.

"I got the sizes you said," Evelyn said. "But you should still try them on. Size is a peculiar thing in Whimsy. One minute I find myself to be an extra-large and then I'm a small again."

"That sounds fascinating," I said.

19

CRASHING THE MASKED BALL

"How are you going to pay for this?" Evelyn asked after we stepped out of the dressing room a few minutes later and now stood by the register while our previous clothes were tucked inside a bag that she gave us.

Enzo's cheeks flushed. "We don't have money."

"I see," Evelyn said.

Enzo picked at his nail. "Is that gonna be a problem?"

Evelyn's smile widened. "Nope. Everything will be fine. We offer stamp credit."

"And what's that?" Enzo asked.

"Our shop lets customers borrow things if they bring them back within 24 hours. We even stamp the customer's wrist to make it official." Evelyn scratched her head.

Being surprised would've only wasted time, because this was Whimsy. That meant it was better to accept whatever crazy fact somebody said, as opposed to arguing its merit. There was no reason for my head to explode, after all.

"What's the catch?" I asked.

Evelyn giggled. "Good question, because there is a catch. People are forced to work for 100 years in the store if said item isn't returned."

Enzo's jaw twitched. "Has anyone ever faced that fate?"

"Only a handful of people," Evelyn said. "Most people are quite responsible. Although there's no reason for two responsible guys like yourself to worry."

Enzo and I looked at each other for a moment. I nodded my head at him because we didn't have a choice. It wasn't like money could be wished all of the sudden. I still had my memory and could recall how money was one of the few things that couldn't be "mixed" with magic.

Enzo pursed his lip. "We'll do the stamp credit."

"Fantastic! Because there really is no reason to be frightened." Evelyn grabbed the stamp pad and stamper after pointing to her wrist.

Enzo and I rolled back one of our sleeves. She stamped Enzo before stamping me. I sniffed the air for a beat, trying to figure out what the stamp smelled like. There was something both sweet and tart to the odor. Almost as if it had a faint peach smell.

"One more question," Enzo said.

Evelyn's eyes lit up. "Sure."

"How far are we from the castle?" Enzo asked.

"Only a mile or two north. Anyway, please tell Queen Bubbles I said hi if you see her," Evelyn squealed.

I frowned. "Do you know her or something?"

"No. But I'm her biggest fan. She inspired me to dye my hair pink." Evelyn wrapped a strand of her hair around her finger. Or as much as she could-considering how there was more hair than finger.

"Will do," I interrupted. "Now we really must be going."

"Have a great day," Evelyn said. "But please remember that the most important thing is for you to bring back the clothes and masks."

I opened the door, and Enzo and I then stepped outside while he continued holding the bag.

I turned to Enzo. "How are we supposed to get to the castle? I've always had a terrible sense of direction."

Enzo laughed. "You don't say."

"It's not funny. Although Mother always hoped I would be a cartographer someday, even though she knew I was directionally challenged."

Mother. It was an interesting word because my memories of her were even shakier than of Father. But I had to remember her because she didn't deserve to be forgotten despite how death stole her from me.

Enzo rubbed a piece of dirt off his half mask, which ran down the left side of his face. "That's a nice way of putting it."

"Do you have any bright ideas, genius?" I asked.

Enzo exhaled a breath. "We can try flying."

"That sounds dangerous."

"It's the only thing we've got. It's not like we have a horse and carriage." Enzo closed his eyes before levitating in the sky. He then zoomed around in circles several times after ascending a few hundred feet in altitude. "Come on. Give it a try."

I whimpered. "Please don't make me fly. I could fall and die."

Enzo now sat a few feet above me midair. "Just give it a try. For me?"

I frowned. "No, I can't."

"Fine. But you can't always use no for an answer." Enzo extended his arm and grabbed my hand before I could even respond to his statement.

My heart pounded a million times faster while the wind slapped my face as we flew through the air. Although it was a nice day for flying because there wasn't a single cloud in the sky.

Time for a confession. Flying made every cell in my body become electrified. Excitement existed from doing something new and dangerous, even if I complained about the risks moments earlier. But I wouldn't tell Enzo how I really felt. I couldn't give him the satisfaction of being right. Not about flying.

We flew through the air as the capital city now only resembled tiny dots on the ground, which meant Enzo must have ascended even higher in altitude when I wasn't paying attention.

Enzo and I soon passed by clusters of trees while the wind still whipped my face.

A brownish-grey castle stood in the distance. But there was a wooden bridge connected to the grass, since there was a lake before the structure. In fact, the copious number of trees near the castle were even reflected on the lake water while sunlight sprinkled down from the sky.

He dived down, and sweat dripped down my back. Although Enzo wasn't as smart as he thought he was. He should have perfected landing as a result of how he thumped against the saturated grass.

Enzo offered me his hand after he grabbed the bag and stood.

We turned our bodies, discovering we weren't alone. Dozens of other masked people in dresses and tuxedoes stood near the castle's front door.

"It'd be nice if the door opened. It's past noon," mumbled a voice.

"Queen Bubbles's parties never start on time," said someone.

Something crackled through the air before the screeching of a bird I was all too familiar made me cover my ears.

Great. Pegasus's reappearance was what Enzo and I needed to feel relaxed. NOT. Although it was a miracle he hadn't reappeared sooner. Because that blasted peacock would have angered even the calmest person.

"What are you doing here, Pegasus?" I asked.

"I was bored." Pegasus continued hovering in midair with his tail spread out in that familiar fan shape. "What about you two?"

"We're going to the masked ball," Enzo said.

Pegasus snorted. "You two were invited to the masked ball?"

I huffed at Pegasus. "Not exactly."

Pegasus glided back and forth through the air. "You two should leave, now ... Queen Bubbles doesn't take kindly to rude people. And she has a temper."

My eyes bulged up. "And how would you know that?"

"You have to trust me." A fog covered Pegasus, and he was gone as fast as he arrived.

Please. Enzo and I didn't have to do anything that blasted peacock said. And no. I wasn't being mean. I was being practical. Pegasus proved his helpfulness a long time ago, and I so looked forward to getting into more trouble because of him.

"That was rather unfortunate," Enzo said.

Trumpets honked before the front door opened. Everyone shuffled into the castle's lobby. We followed the people and were able to get inside. A carpet cloaked the floor and there were tables of food and beverages while harp music echoed in the background from somewhere nearby.

"Do you want to dance or eat first?" Enzo asked.

I shrugged. "I don't care."

Someone tapped my back. "Excuse me, but I don't recall children being on the guest list."

Enzo and I spun around.

A man in a tunic, pants, and boots who had salt and pepper colored hair and a mustache stood before us. He also happened to be holding a bayonet.

"It's a funny story," Enzo stammered.

"I'm sure it is," he said, "But you must come with me to a detention room. There's no doubt Queen Bubbles will want to talk to you herself. Now you can either come willingly, or I can drag you."

Ficklewamper. Ficklewamper. Ficklewamper. That blasted peacock just had to be right about how showing up uninvited to the party was dumb. Although having a good time was nice while the idea lasted. I couldn't fault Enzo for wanting to cheer me up, no matter how problematic his moment of serendipity was for us.

20

MEETING QUEEN BUBBLES

"I'm so sorry, Alex. I didn't realize we would get in trouble." Enzo gave me a sorrowful look while we sat at a wooden table in a room, which couldn't have been bigger than the size of my bedroom.

I rested my right hand under my chin. "Don't worry about it. Let's just hope we don't lose our heads."

"I'm sure everything will be fine." Enzo squeezed my hand.

Yelling at Enzo for telling me what I wanted to hear would have been pointless. People sometimes needed comfort over reality. But maybe, just maybe, life would be okay. It had to be. And no. I wasn't trying to complain. I had my whole life ahead of me, and didn't deserve to have it cut short by one moment of foolishness.

I sucked in a breath. "I hope so. You know what will happen to us if we don't return the masks and outfits."

Yup. I was a lot of things, but being ignoring the stamp credit situation wouldn't happen. Only an idiot would have been cavalier about a hundred years of shop work because of failing to return the items to the store.

The door opened, and we tilted our heads. A woman with a crown and pink hair shuffled into the room. She had a long-sleeved dress, which extended to her ankles. She also had a staff she gripped with her right hand, as if her life depended on it. And no. I wasn't exaggerating since the wooden staff would have shattered if she held it any tighter.

The door's slamming vibrated throughout the room as she made her way over to Enzo and me before standing directly in front of the table. Although she didn't have a mask on, which seemed strange. Today was the masked ball. Then again, she could have taken her mask off before coming here.

Queen Bubbles screamed. "You have no idea how much I was looking forward to today's festivities before you interrupted them!"

Enzo and I exchanged a quick glance. But we didn't have to be psychic to know what the other thought because we could either speak or remain silent. However, there was no telling how Queen Bubbles would react since we didn't know anything about her other than what Pegasus told us.

"You could at least respond. It's rude to ignore the queen." Queen Bubbles pounded her free hand on the table after making a fist.

Ficklewamper. Pegasus might have been a lot of things, but I couldn't get mad at him for warning us about Queen Bubbles's temper. Although it would have been nice if he weren't correct because avoiding Ramona was already problem enough.

I exhaled a breath. "We didn't mean any offense, Your Majesty."

Queen Bubbles clenched her jaw. "That's what they all say."

"Can we go?" Enzo asked.

"I'll ask the questions," Queen Bubbles said.

I shook my head. Our situation was bad enough without Queen Bubbles taking offense to something he said. But maybe, just maybe, Enzo and I would get out of this predicament unscathed. We had to since enough bad and complicated things happened already.

Enzo's jaw trembled. "Are we going to lose our heads?"

"I said I'll ask the questions!" Queen Bubbles yelled even louder this time. "Anyway, what were you doing at the masked ball in the first place? Don't you know only adults are invited?"

Honesty might have been risky, but it was the only move left. Remaining silent would have angered Queen Bubbles. Besides, there was a chance she could feel sorry for us despite how steam would have oozed out of her head if she got any angrier.

I hung my head lower. "It's a complicated story."

Queen Bubbles gave us a warm look. "I like stories. And you might as well tell because we have all the time in the world."

Enzo shot me a glance. "Are you sure telling her is right?"

Figures. Enzo just had to have the opposite opinion of me.

I lifted my gaze off the table and towards Queen Bubbles. "I ran away from Flimsy because my stepmother tried to kill me. She wants my rubies my father left for me, and I made a deal with a magic to retrieve a crystal from the Kuku mountains to help defeat her if I succeed with his quest."

Queen Bubbles furrowed an eyebrow. "You're a long way from the Kuku mountains."

"Don't get mad at Alex, Your Majesty," Enzo said. "Going to the masked ball was my idea. He even tried talking me out of it. I just thought it would be nice to have a little fun."

Defending me was nice. But I would have to hope that Queen Bubbles didn't get even angrier. Admitting I tried talking Enzo out of party crashing meant we did the "wrong" thing, anyway.

A vein surfaced on Queen Bubbles's head. "You wouldn't have to know anything about the gingerbread house incident, would you? King Fabio of the flamingos told me someone tried to steal gumdrops from there."

Selling the story meant I couldn't even take in a couple of deep breaths because any hesitation would out me. "Of course not. Enzo and I would never break any rules."

I continued shivering despite wearing Enzo's jacket—a cold dampness permeated the air. Although icy sensations shooting up my body were the least of my problem. We were still no closer to getting our freedom.

My lips curled. "What are you going to, Your Majesty?"

"I normally loathe children, in addition to how I hate when my parties are interrupted," Queen Bubbles said. "But I'll make an exception because I have a son a couple of years older than you guys."

Enzo nodded. "Thank you. We'll get out of your way and won't be a problem any longer."

Queen Bubbles waved her free hand through the air. "Nonsense. You'll rest here for a few days and then you can take one of my pet dragons to the Kuku mountains."

"We wouldn't want to be any trouble," I said.

Queen Bubbles rubbed her crown, accentuating its gold texture. "You wouldn't be arguing with me, would you?"

I coughed. "Of course not. I would never dream of offending you."

"Relax," Queen Bubbles said. "I was joking. But I was serious about giving you lodging. I pride myself on being a good hostess and would hate for someone to think I'm rude."

"We have a slight problem, Your Majesty," I said. "We have to return these outfits and masks to a shop in the capital city because we bought them using stamp credit."

Queen Bubbles's laughter echoed through the room. "No worries. I can have someone run the errand for you. Now, what do you say we get out of this dismal room?"

Please. Queen Bubbles didn't just refer to this room as dismal. It wasn't like she was a guest in someone else's castle. This was her domain, and she should have known what the room looked like. She also should have done something about the room if she didn't like it. Being passive made people seem weak, and that was no way to live life. At least in my opinion. I couldn't speak for everyone else, no matter how tempting that was.

"You can freshen up and get pampered with all your favorite foods," Queen Bubbles continued. "No offense or anything, but you two look like skeletons. Do your parents feed you enough?"

Hmmm. Perhaps Queen Bubbles wasn't terrible. Going off on a tangent by inventing a problem meant we might have had more in common than I realized.

A lump lingered in my throat. "We're both orphans."

"Very well," Queen Bubble said. "But let's get a move on. I hate wasting time, because it makes me so angry."

Ficklewamper. Queen Bubbles must have misspoken. She was the one wasting time by making a production for every thought she had. But Whatever. I couldn't judge her. Not when my head throbbed from how my life was still chaotic.

21

MARINO'S WARNING

I knocked on Enzo's room sometime later after taking a shower, which was the best thing ever.

Sure. We might have been on an important mission, in addition to how it would have been awkward to bring up hygiene in front of Enzo. But nothing would change the comfort of warm water splashing out of the shower head and onto my body. There was only so much longer I could have gone around with a sweaty body.

"Come in," Enzo said.

I shuffled into Enzo's room, which couldn't have been more than twenty by twenty feet. It consisted of a bed, table, bathroom, and window, which overlooked a luscious forest outside.

"Help yourself to any of the food that was brought up," Enzo continued.

My attention shifted back to the table where various plates of pastries, such as cookies, cupcakes, brownies, and candy were in addition to a couple of plates of pasta and chicken. A pitcher of water also sat in the center of the table.

I rubbed my hands together. "It all looks so good."

"I don't even know where to start."

A strawberry scent wafted through the air.

"I see you got the fruit shampoo too?" I asked.

He nodded. "Yup."

I chuckled. "Father would scold me if he were still alive, but I don't care. I'm starting with dessert first."

"Sounds great."

Enzo and I grabbed some cupcakes. The cake part of the cupcake was so moist that I didn't need water to wash it down, even though the sweet taste of the frosting lingering in my mouth almost overpowered me.

Enzo drew in a breath. "How scared were you?"

"Excuse me?"

"You don't have to hide your feelings, Alex."

"I thought we were going to lose our heads."

He took one of the cups that was on the table before grabbing the pitcher and filling it all the way to the top with water. "I'm impressed with how well you handled yourself in front of Queen Bubbles," he said.

My cheeks flushed. "You don't have to compliment me."

"It's the truth." Enzo finished his water and poured himself a refill.

"We shouldn't be surprised about how Queen Bubbles offered us shelter."

"And why is that?"

I laughed even louder this time. "Everything is backwards in Whimsy."

He smirked. "That's true."

"Although I would hate to see Queen Bubbles really mad."

"You and me both."

An itch shot up my nose, and I scratched it. "Can I ask you a question?"

Enzo wiggled a finger at me. "Ask me whatever you want. You don't need my permission."

"Do you still miss Hanna?"

Pink, purple, orange, and blue were mixed together in the sky outside, while the faint outline of several clouds remained visible.

Wow. Today had gone by faster than I realized if it was already twilight. But that wasn't bad even if time always escaped me. Only a fool would have been oblivious to how today was beyond taxing.

I bit my lip. "It's okay. You don't have to answer my question if you don't want to."

He munched on another cookie. "I just hope this detour hasn't delayed our mission too much."

"Our" might have been a simple word because it only had three letters. But the truth was in the subtext. Using that word meant Enzo took ownership of the mission and linked us together. And that was more than a little detail, because I had another confession to make. Enzo might have been a nice person, but a part of me couldn't help but almost lower my jaw at how Enzo hadn't lost interest in our adventure. I wasn't even trying to invent a problem, though, since accompanying me through Whimsy asked a lot of him.

So, yeah. Hanna might have betrayed us. But she would have never had done that if Enzo never accompanied me to Whimsy. Now wasn't the time to consider every possible facet of a situation. I could either have an internal dialogue with myself or enjoy having quality time with Enzo.

"I wish we could stay here forever," I said without even thinking about the ramifications of my comment.

He blinked. "Come again?"

"It's nice here. It certainly is better than trekking our way through Whimsy."

He quirked his eyebrows. "You're the one who wanted to come here in the first place."

"I'm serious. Our lives would be perfect if Queen Bubbles let us live here forever," I said.

Enzo put his hands on his hips. "You can't avoid your stepmother."

"I know, but it's a nice fantasy."

"I suppose you have a point."

"But then everything will have been for nothing."

"Whimsy is kind of nice." Enzo got a brownie and devoured it in a matter of seconds.

I locked my fingers together. "I know I must sound a little eccentric."

He waved his hand through the air. "It's okay. Don't worry about it. It's part of your charm."

I scratched my chin. "I wonder what Pegasus would say if he were here."

Enzo's eyes lit up. "I thought you didn't like Pegasus?"

"He's still humorous, even if he's annoying."

"Do you want to stay here?" Enzo asked.

My shoulders buoyed up. "I don't know. It would solve a lot of our problems."

Staying in Whimsy wasn't only an idealistic sentiment. It was comforting because the stories Mother used to read me before bed still remained etched in my mind.

Sure. The particular details of all the tales might have been blurred. However, the characters who ventured into neighboring fantasy lands always seemed to despise the journey and wanted nothing more than to return home. But not me. At least not anymore. Or maybe that was the sugar talking, because that was a strong possibility. Sugar made even the most impractical idea seem genius.

Enzo sighed. "We can ask Queen Bubbles to stay here if you really want to. But you have to be sure of what you want."

A burning sensation stung my neck, making me touch the pendant part of the necklace, which Marino the Great had given me. The steam from feeling the necklace made me blow air on my finger.

"Do you mind if I use the bathroom for a second?" I asked while the pedant continued scorching my skin.

Enzo pointed to the bathroom. "Not at all. Help yourself."

I scurried into the bathroom, and couldn't have shut the door any faster if I tried. I took the necklace off and gripped it by the part that attached itself to my neck so I wouldn't be burned.

"I'm sorry I burned you … I just had to get your attention," mumbled a voice.

I glanced down at the necklace, only to be greeted by the appearance of the man on the pendant.

"I didn't realize this was a two-way mirror?" I asked, after turning the faucet on and letting water splash into the sink so Enzo wouldn't be able to hear my conversation.

"It's an insurance policy," Marino said.

I grunted. "What do you want?"

"I don't think that's any way to talk to the person who will help you defeat your stepmother. But I'll ignore your rudeness since we both need each other."

I rolled my eyes. "You never said you would check up on me."

"Well, I am. And there's not much you can do about it."

Yup. I had more than enough reason to feel like something acidic stung my mouth. I was twelve years old, not a five-year-old. And that meant I didn't need the man to check up on me. I was capable of going to the Kuku mountains and getting the crystal he wanted. Doing so would just take more time than I anticipated, since Whimsy was anything but simple. That was if I wanted to complete the mission. I still stood by my earlier statement about how staying in Whimsy would be easier than duking it out with Ramona. Although she found me once so there was a chance that she could find me again. I mean, she might have been trapped. But she wasn't gone for good.

Hmmm. If only I could remember that word one of my teachers taught me in school. Oh, yeah. The word was "hubris." Anyway, my point was I wouldn't get arrogant, even if having a reprieve from Ramona was enjoyable. She might have been a lot of things, but she wasn't stupid.

"I asked you a question ... How are things going?" Marino asked.

"I actually need to talk to you about that," I said, trying not to stutter.

"Don't tell me you're in danger?"

"Nothing like that."

"Then what?" Marino asked.

I counted to twenty in my head—my response required careful phrasing. Getting the man mad was the last thing I needed, after all. "Would you really be so mad if I didn't want to go through the mission?"

The man grunted. "Where is this coming from?"

"I don't know. It's complicated."

Marino remained silent for a beat. "This isn't what we agreed to..."

I gritted my teeth. "I know. But Whimsy isn't as bad as it seems. Seeking refuge in here might be the safest bet."

"I said I honor my deals."

"What's your point?" I spat.

Marino grunted. "Let me finish. Yes. I do honor my deals. However, you don't want to know what happens when someone double crosses me."

"What are you going to do? Make me work for free for the next 100 years? Besides, aren't you dying?"

"Yes. But I'm not gone yet."

"Goodbye. I'm done, and am no longer interested in sparring with my stepmother," I said.

Marino the Great's image disappeared from the pendant, as did the scorching sensation. I then put it back on my neck before turning off the sink faucet and opening the door.

And no. Putting the necklace back on me wasn't dumb, even if I backed out of my pact. I couldn't let anyone else find it.

Enzo looked up from the table. "No offense or anything, but you were in the bathroom a long time."

"I've made up my mind. I wanna stay in Whimsy."

Yeah. I was certain of my decision, regardless of how my stomach just twisted in ten different directions. It wasn't like Marino the Great could do anything terrible to Enzo and me since he was in Flimsy. I hoped not, at least.

22

A REQUEST

Sunlight trickled into my bedroom the following morning. Birds chirped, then I rubbed my eyes and yawned.

Being tired couldn't be helped, regardless of how Queen Bubbles provided me shelter. Worrying was sometimes justified, even if it could be problematic. Waiting a few more minutes to open my eyes would have been good, though, since Pegasus's latest appearance wasn't something that I needed to deal with today. Thinking about what the man would do to me because I wanted to break the deal was more than enough to make tingling sensations crawl up my back.

"What are you doing here?" I screamed.

Pegasus expanded its tail into a fan shape while hovering in the air before me. "I just wanted to say hi."

"Don't you have anything better to do?"

"I'm all out of blue fizz."

"You shouldn't be drinking blue fizz if it's morning, you fool." I got out of bed and stretched.

Pegasus munched on something. "I'm not an idiot. I would never drink blue fizz in the morning. I was talking about last night."

I scrunched my eyebrows. "Whatever. I don't care."

"I'm sure you care more than you realize. I would like to think we're friends."

I snorted. It didn't matter if it was too early to be combative. Some ideas were just that outrageous. "I don't even know anything about you other than a couple of your associates."

Pegasus cawed at me. "Oh, yes. I wonder how Francis is. I should keep in touch with him more often."

"I probably shouldn't be telling you this, but I've decided to stay in Whimsy."

"That's interesting," Pegasus said.

I folded my arms. "I'm serious. Whimsy is much better than Flimsy."

"Whatever makes you happy. Just make sure this is what you want, since decisions can haunt you even years down the line." A crackling sound swooshed through the air before a mist covered Pegasus. He was gone when it cleared.

Someone knocked on my door, and I hurried over to see who was at the door.

"Queen Bubbles would be honored if you and your friend joined her for breakfast in ten minutes," said one of the queen's servants. She sported a pink tunic, pants, and shoes. Plus, her hair was divided into two braids.

"It's kinda short notice."

She glared; eyes filled with mild contempt. "Attendance is mandatory. Besides, you don't want to make the queen angry."

"If you insist. Goodbye." I closed the door and headed towards the bathroom so I could wash my face.

My stomach tightened. Apparently, the lump in my throat would never go away, regardless of how many times I got out of trouble. Or maybe there was something about Queen Bubbles's temper that terrified me. But I would have to get used to my insides fluttering if I wanted to stay here. That was if Queen Bubbles let me stay, since she could kick Enzo and me out of the castle on a moment's notice. Because Royalty was nothing to look down on. Something intimidating still existed about royalty because of the implied formalities. At least in my opinion. I still remembered the tale Father read to me involving a queen who kicked everyone out of the castle for never using proper etiquette.

Whatever. I could think about that story later if I wanted to. I had to finish washing my face in my bathroom since I didn't want to risk angering Queen Bubbles by arriving late to breakfast. Although beheading someone for tardiness seemed excessive.

23

OFF WITH YOUR HEAD

"Thank you so much for inviting us to breakfast, Your Majesty." I sat next to Enzo in the dining room.

A silk tablecloth covered the table, and each person had a plate, spoon, fork, knife, napkin, and a glass of juice and water. The meal was buffet style, since a bunch of choices sat on the table. There were also two candles—that smelled like jasmine—on the center of the table, with flames flickering out of them.

The candles seemed a bit much, though. The electricity worked fine, just like in Flimsy, which was evident by the lights being on. Then again, Queen Bubbles probably just wanted to add atmosphere to the meal.

Queen Bubbles banged her fist on the table. "I've changed my mind—enough of this Your Majesty nonsense. You may call me Bubbles."

I nodded. "Of course."

"Plus, I thought it would be nice if you met Captain Rickshaw." Queen Bubbles rubbed her hands together.

Oops. I almost forgot to mention how there was a fourth person at the table. A certain Captain Rickshaw who sported a pink uniform and hat. He was the one of the most prominent people in Queen Bubbles's royal circle and had just come back from fending off the ogres in the south.

Enzo grabbed one of the platters and put several pancakes on his plate before taking a sliver of butter and drowning his meal in syrup. "Where are your son and husband, Bubbles?"

I glared at Enzo. He should have known better than to ask a nosy question. After all, we hadn't even been in the castle a full day yet.

Queen Bubbles made a fist. "I don't talk about my husband. Well, ex-husband now. But semantics doesn't matter."

"Did he lose his head?" Enzo asked.

I clapped my hand over my head because Enzo knew all the right questions to ask. NOT. Nothing bad had happened to us yet, though. So, maybe, just maybe, Queen Bubbles would cut us slack and indulge our curiosity since we were children.

Queen Bubbles giggled. "Don't be ridiculous, child. I just banished him to the East and let my son see him every other year."

Enzo poured more syrup on his food. "Where is your son?"

"On an educational field trip with his tutor. But he'll be back in a couple of weeks. Although I do hope he doesn't get into any trouble. His mind has a tendency to wander." Queen Bubbles drank some of her juice.

I broke off a piece of sausage into a smaller bite before devouring it. The mixture of the spicy, meat, and sweet flavors jolted my tongue. The taste even lingered in my mouth for a beat. "You must miss your son, Bubbles," I said.

Queen Bubbles didn't respond. Instead, frown lines formed on her face as a result of a fly continuing to buzz near her head. And I would have laughed in any other context. But no. Something about the violent red color on her cheeks told me that Queen Bubbles was in no mood to be smacked.

"There! I got it!" Queen Bubbles just squashed the bug in one swift motion.

"I'm glad to be back from the south," Captain Rickshaw added.

"Me too," Queen Bubbles squealed. "Now you can go back to working castle security. Because I have a confession to make, Rickshaw."

Captain Rickshaw arched his eyebrow. "And what would that be?"

"I haven't felt safe in your absence. But hopefully those pesky ogres will behave themselves, otherwise they'll be the next ones to lose their heads." Queen Bubbles waved her knife through the air.

Water fell out of my nose because Queen Bubbles actually referred to beheadings out loud as opposed to only alluding to it. "What did the ogres do?"

Her eyes bulged up. "What did they do? Well, let's see. They've been terrorizing villagers even though they are supposed to stay in the Forfor Forest."

I fanned myself with my shirt. "How dreadful. I'm sorry to hear that."

"It doesn't matter now. Anyway, as I was saying, you have no idea how worried I was, Rickshaw. In fact, these two rascals snuck into the masked ball the other day."

Captain Rickshaw looked down at his plate. "The horrors."

"But I'm fine now. They explained their situation, and I was happy to help them. I do pride myself in being a generous person." Queen Bubbles scooped more eggs onto her plate.

Captain Rickshaw grinned. "You're the most generous person I know."

Queen Bubbles pressed her hand over her chest. "Thank you. That means more than you can ever know."

Okay. Maybe Enzo was right, even if I didn't want to exactly admit that to myself. Breakfast was going fine since nobody had lost his or her head yet, besides how the conversation was pleasant as opposed to being forced. And it was even interesting to soak up more information about Whimsy. Although I would have to keep one thing to myself because it didn't seem appropriate to tell Queen Bubbles that she should have been more proactive if she was so concerned about castle security. But that was my opinion because some things weren't worth fighting about.

Queen Bubbles glanced at me. "You're awfully quiet, child. Is something wrong with the food? I can give the chef a stern talking to if you like."

Good graciousness. Queen Bubbles was always on edge because she could never take a moment to just breathe. In fact, I'd even go as far as to say she made me look formal.

My jaw twitched. "That won't be necessary. I just like to think before I speak."

Queen Bubbles swirled her glass around in circles before finishing the rest of her juice. "That's a wonderful idea. I can't tell you how many times I meet people who don't think before speaking."

Enzo winked at her. "What happens to them?"

Queen Bubbles cracked her knuckles. "I smack sense into them. At least with the people who haven't lost their heads."

A burning sensation spread through my neck before I glanced down at the pendant. Marino the Great's image was back.

Marino the Great whispered, "You will insult Queen Bubbles in the hopes of getting into trouble."

The heat pressing against my flesh vanished, as did Marino's image.

"Everything okay, Alex?" Enzo finished the rest of his pancakes.

The fork fell from my hand and banged against the table. "Nope. It isn't. I'm sorry, but I think you're the biggest moron in the world, Bubbles."

Queen Bubbles pressed against her water glass so tight that it shattered into a bunch of fragments before the shards scattered onto the tablecloth. "What did you just say, child?"

"I said you're the biggest moron because you're nothing but a lazy despotic ruler. You complain about your security yet you didn't do anything about it even though you knew Captain Rickshaw would be out of the castle. It's pretty dumb if you ask me. Inspiring fear in people will only get you so far. But if you want to take the easy way, then so be it." I laughed at Queen Bubbles. My tone was so manic that I'd go as far as to say my chuckling resembled a hyena.

Enzo bit his lip. "Are you feeling okay, Alex? Maybe you need to lie down?"

"Nope," I said. "I'm fine and have no doubts about what I said. I mean, Bubbles is kind of a ridiculous name."

Captain Rickshaw feigned a smile. "I think rest is a great idea. The boy might have a case of the failures."

Interesting. Captain Rickshaw made an excuse for me even though he didn't know anything about my life. Some people were like that, though. Giving someone the benefit of the doubt required less effort than waging some campaign against someone. Although Queen Bubbles probably would have had the opposite opinion.

Queen Bubbles's face was now redder than a tomato, which made me fill the room with even louder laughter. "Apologize this instance!"

"Nope. You should at least stand up if you want me to apologize." I finished the rest of my food.

Queen Bubbles banged both hands against the table, causing the plates and glasses to rattle. "This is your last chance, child."

The man might have made me say what I did, but I wasn't wrong. At least entirely, anyone should have realized how Queen Bubbles seemed to have a tendency to get angry. And that wasn't a flattering emotion. She was the Queen and should have known better. After all, the people of Whimsy were doomed if they couldn't depend on their queen to illustrate proper etiquette.

Enzo leaned into my ear. "Just apologize. You can say you snuck some blue fizz and don't feel in control."

I tapped my hands on the table. "That would be a lie because I don't make a habit of apologizing to a queen who deserves the title of Court Jester."

Queen Bubbles jumped out of her chair, pointing her right index finger. "That's it. Off with your head."

24

PEGASUS THE LAWYER

"Thank you for agreeing to be my lawyer, Pegasus," I sat next to Enzo at a table in the interrogation room we were first in after one of Queen Bubble's guards found us sneaking into the masked ball.

Pegasus lowered his body until he thudded against the wooden table. "No problem. I knew it must have been important when you kept calling my name."

I rolled my eyes. "It was the only thing I could think of. I was just shocked you could hear me from wherever you were."

Enzo flinched. "Please tell us there's some way to get out of this predicament. This is a big misunderstanding."

"I can speak for myself," I spat.

Getting irritated with Enzo might have been the wrong thing to do, but I couldn't help myself. And my reaction had nothing to do with thinking I didn't need help. I needed all the assistance I could get. It was just seeming weak was the last thing I needed right now, though.

Enzo bit his lip. "I was only trying to help."

I took off the necklace. "All I have left is this silly thing. And it's not like I can just summon the man because foreigners can't just poof to random places."

Pegasus used his left claw to rub his right foot. "It's my first time in court."

The trees jerked outside while the wind hissed. There was a window, which meant a view. The wind's echo lingered in the room while I rubbed my hands together in order to create friction so I could get warm.

"What do you know about the Whimsy courts?" I asked.

"It's actually called Kangaroo Court," Pegasus revealed.

Enzo gasped. "Pardon me?"

Pegasus took in a deep breath. "I'm being serious. Whimsy's legal system is called Kangaroo Court. And yes, the judge is an actual kangaroo."

I smiled. "At least Queen Bubbles isn't the judge."

"The judge isn't our problem," Pegasus said. "Queen Bubbles is. She'll be the prosecutor and jury."

"Then what's the point of having a judge?" Enzo asked.

Yup. Enzo wasn't the only one scratching his head. Everything about Whimsy got more bizarre with each passing moment. Almost like the country made up its rules as it went along. But now wasn't the time to think about how a country as illogical as Whimsy could exist. Not when my freedom was dubious.

"To maintain order in the courtroom," Pegasus said. "Killian is more of a figurehead, though, because he'll sit at the prosecution's table while Queen Bubbles sits in the judge's seat with the gavel. But don't worry. We'll be sitting at the defense table."

I grunted. "I don't think that will help us."

Enzo recoiled. "How are we supposed to win the trial if Queen Bubbles is the prosecution and jury?"

Pegasus hung his head lower. "I'm afraid the trial is more of a formality since she's only ever sided with the defense once."

I averted my gaze. "That's great."

Enzo beamed. "At least tell me you have a good strategy."

"Good question, Enzo," Pegasus said. "But the defense isn't allowed to present evidence at the trial."

I sobbed. Getting upset was the only thing worth doing. I was stupid because I thought I could defy Marino the Great without any consequences. But apparently life had other plans for me, and there wasn't a darn thing I could do about.

"Then what's the point of us even being there?" I wiped the tears away.

"To save face," Pegasus said.

I cried louder this time. "Is there anything we can do?"

Pegasus didn't respond. At least not at first. But his silence was for the best. There was a good chance his reply might have irritated me because he wasn't tactful.

"There might be one thing, but it's a bit of a wild card," Pegasus finally said.

"I'm surprised it's taking so long," Enzo said.

"Queen Bubbles is just gathering the witnesses," Pegasus said.

I put my hand under my chin. "Wonderful. What a surprise."

My situation might have been far from ideal. But there had to be a way out of my current predicament. Sure. Whimsy was a backwards place. However, I somehow made it this far and it would be a shame if I stopped in my tracks now.

Enzo's Adam's apple throbbed. "How does Queen Bubbles even know what witnesses to call?"

"I'm not sure I want the answer," I interrupted.

"Invisible bugs are everywhere in Whimsy and collect data on every foreigner that enters the country," Pegasus revealed. "The recordings go into some giant machine, but

Queen Bubbles only looks at it when it's relevant to a trial."

My jaw quaked. "They'll know what we've been up to this whole time?"

Pegasus nodded. "I'm afraid so."

Okay. Whimsy once again got even weirder. And that was the last thing I wanted or needed. It was hard to win the game if the rules kept changing at moment's notice. It wasn't unreasonable to think I deserved a fair chance, after all.

25

THE TRIAL

The trial began sometime later. The arrangement was what Pegasus said it would be like. Queen Bubbles sat in the judge's chair with her gavel while Killian the kangaroo sat at the left table, and Pegasus, Enzo, and I sat at the right mahogany table. But it wasn't just the five of us. There wasn't even one free seat in the courtroom, which was in the castle. Although at least the tables were a few hundred feet away from Queen Bubbles, which was about the only positive thing I could hold onto.

And no. I wasn't grasping at straws by being thankful there was a good distance between my table and Queen Bubble's table. Not being close to Queen Bubbles meant she couldn't physically do anything to me. At least for the moment.

Queen Bubbles banged her gavel. "The defendant is charged with slander, libel, and intent to cause me great emotional harm. How do you plead, Alex?"

I rose. "Not guilty, Your Majesty."

Queen Bubbles turned the court stenographer, which was a monkey sitting in a chair with a notepad and pen. "Let the record show the defendant has pled guilty, and I'm only granting this trial out of mercy and pity."

I stood up again. "I said, 'not guilty.'"

"Be quiet!" Queen Bubbles slammed her gavel several more times.

"Time for the first witness!" Queen Bubbles exclaimed.

The courtroom door opened, and one of Queen Bubble's guards escorted Captain Rickshaw to the witness stand.

"What do you know about the incident?" Queen Bubbles asked after Captain Rickshaw sat down on the witness stand.

Captain Rickshaw rubbed his mustache. "He insulted Your Majesty's name and implied your incompetence multiple times. You even offered to forgive if he apologized, but he was vicious. I've never seen such a more brutal defamation. But worst of all was that he thought you deserved the title of royal jester."

Good gracious. Rage pulsed through my entire body, yet I couldn't get mad at Captain Rickshaw. He told the truth as opposed to lying, which meant he was an honorable person. Although I shouldn't have been defending Captain Rickshaw's testimony against me since I was still no closer to escaping this ridiculous situation.

The courtroom broke out into dozens of gasps before Queen Bubbles smacked the gavel several times. "Silence!" Queen Bubbles screamed.

"What do you know about Alex?" Queen Bubbles asked King Fabio of the flamingos after he took the stand.

"He took the gumdrops from the gingerbread house," King Fabio said.

Queen Bubbles pushed her crown up with her free hand. "Let the record reflect I'm adding dozens of additional charges."

The monkey nodded at Queen Bubbles.

Okay. Queen Bubbles's action was awful. It would have been nice if you did me the courtesy of knowing what those charges were. But no. Having transparency was too difficult for you and everything had to be masked in logical fallacies.

Smith shuffled into the courtroom next and took the stand.

"What can you tell the court about this dreadful young man?" Queen Bubbles demanded.

"He broke into my shop and tried to rob it, so I let him take all the money from the register." Smith took out a handkerchief and blew his nose.

I stood up without even thinking because I might as well have defended myself if I would lose my head. "That's a lie. He willingly gave Enzo and I two rings."

Enzo got up too and pointed to his ring. But I didn't have time to think about Enzo being on my side. Not when the trial had turned into a farce. King Fabio's and Captain Rickshaw's testimony was one thing. But it was another thing to go along with a psychotic queen by fabricating a story.

Queen Bubbles banged the gavel so hard and fast that I almost thought it'd break this time. "Please be quiet or I'll be forced to add twenty more charges."

Smith shuffled out of court before Francis strutted into the courtroom.

Hmmm. Maybe there was a chance Francis would say something nice since I defeated the kraken and he owed me a great debt. Thinking Francis would help was probably foolish. My trial wasn't going well, and it was hard to think things would improve.

Queen Bubbles's eyes lit up. "What can you tell us about this dangerous delinquent?"

Ficklewamper. Being illogical was one thing. But Queen Bubbles should have known better than to interject her own opinion. She wasn't testifying.

Francis got a cloth from his pocket, but he didn't blow his nose like Smith had. Instead, he rubbed his eyes instead. He then put the cloth back into his jacket pocket before stealing a brief glance at me and mouthing, "I'm sorry."

"He killed my pet kraken for no reason," Francis said. "His name was Carlyle, and he didn't pose a threat to the lad."

Queen Bubbles gripped both sides of her head. "Unbelievable."

"That's a lie, Your Majesty," I said without even bothering to stand. There was no doubt Queen Bubbles would just yell at me. "The so-called kraken killed his wife and daughter. I actually did him a favor,".

Queen Bubbles's pupils dilated. "This is your last warning, brat! You'll lose your head if you say one more word without my permission. Do you understand?"

I nodded.

"I asked you a question," Queen Bubbles said.

Sweat tumbled down my face while my pulse blasted in my ears. There was no safe answer to Queen Bubbles's question. It could have been a trap, which meant I would get in trouble for talking. Although it could have been genuine too and there was a chance of getting in trouble if I didn't respond.

Hmmm. Decisions. Decisions.

I exhaled a long breath. "Yes. I understand, Your Majesty."

Queen Bubbles grinned. "That was a trick question. But the trial is almost done, and I have nothing better to do. So, I'll be generous and let your mistake slide. Although I won't be forgiving next time."

Enzo gripped my hand, making my pulse beat a little slower. A simple gesture of support was about the only thing I could hold onto right now.

"What do you know about Alex?" Queen Bubbles asked Evelyn after she took the stand.

Evelyn took out her hair tie and let her hair bounce down from a tight wrapped bun as her hair now reached the same long point as before. "He borrowed something on stamp credit without even returning the item. I then went to see him about it, and Alex threatened to kill me if I made him work for 100 years."

Standing up and pointing out the latest lie would have been a waste of breath because there was no changing a stubborn person.

"I'm sorry, dear." Queen Bubble whipped her head back and forth.

I sniffed the air for a second while something wafted through the air. Figures. I was so distracted by the "trial" that I forgot how the air smelled like pinewood. Whatever.

No use in complaining about the odor because it wouldn't grant me my freedom.

"I've come to a decision," Queen Bubbles said the second Evelyn stepped out of the courtroom and the guard slammed the door behind her. "I find you guilty, Alex. You're going to lose your head right now."

"Not so fast, Your Majesty," Pegasus said.

Queen Bubbles pounded the gavel again. "Quiet. I'm speaking."

"I'm afraid Alex isn't going to lose his head just yet," Pegasus said. "Law 34 says a guilty defendant is entitled to an appeal."

"Nobody has ever asked for an appeal before." Queen Bubbles bit one of her fingernails.

"I just did," Pegasus touted.

Queen Bubbles clenched her jaw. "Fine. I'm always down for a bubble blowing tournament."

Wow. Pegasus got me a reprieve despite seeming like a blithering idiot.

I couldn't jump for joy at a non-traditional appeal, though. I couldn't even remember if I ever used one of those home bubble-blowing kits as a kid.

Whatever. Getting an appeal was reason enough to be laughing right now, and I'd take it. I needed something, anything, to hold on to. I refused to die on the whim of a psychotic queen. I was only twelve, after all.

26

BLOWING BUBBLES

Queen Bubbles, Pegasus, Enzo, and I stood in a spot behind the castle along with the monkey, witnesses, and trial audience members. Saturated grey clouds remained stacked together in the sky, begging whether it would rain or snow. And no. I wasn't being too analytical. I was in Whimsy and anyone's guess was as good as mine. One would think it could snow since there was a chill. Although others might have thought it would be the Whimsy thing for it to rain when it was supposed to snow.

"The rules are simple." Queen Bubbles gripped her bubble blowing mix and stick. "Whoever makes the most beautiful bubbles wins."

Good gracious. Blowing bubbles was more than an unconventional method for appealing a guilty verdict. But it wasn't like I could stomp both feet on the ground and demand Queen Bubbles implement logic.

"How am I supposed to blow beautiful bubbles?" I whispered to Pegasus.

Pegasus swatted a fly buzzing nearby with his tail, which was once again in a fan shape. "It's all random."

Enzo clicked his lips together. "That's just what we need."

"Don't despair," Pegasus said. "I've got us this far. We can win. You just have to believe."

I raised an eyebrow. "Was Queen Bubbles always this unstable?"

"No … But that's a matter of another time," Pegasus said.

Queen Bubbles scowled. "What are you three babbling about? Don't you know it's rude to whisper?"

Enzo, Pegasus, and I exchanged a quick glance with each other before casting our gaze elsewhere.

"Whatever. Let's just get on with this because I have a tea party to get to later today." Queen Bubbles twisted the cap off the bubble blowing mix before taking her stick and scooping some of the mix. She blew it out and an opaque dove, tiger, rose, and dog formed before disappearing after a beat.

Couldn't say I was surprised that normal bubbles didn't form. This was Whimsy, after all. The country where anything was possible.

Queen Bubbles's eyes bulged up. "What are you waiting for, child? We don't have all day."

"Sorry, Your Majesty." I removed the mix's cap before taking my stick and scooping the contents. Blowing the mix free from the circular hole made a deer, cherry blossom tree, and two dancing kids appear.

Queen Bubbles rolled her eyes. "Not bad for a beginner. But I'll soon cream you. Just you see."

"Don't listen to her," Enzo mumbled into my ear.

Queen Bubbles waved her stick at us. "I thought I told you whispering is rude?"

She scooped some mix and blew it out of the circle. A kraken, crocodile, and shark formed before a gust of wind popped them in a matter of seconds.

A vein surfaced on Queen Bubbles's head before she cocked her head towards the crowd. "Why aren't you clapping? I just made beautiful bubbles."

Please. The tyrant wasn't fooling anyone because a kraken, crocodile, and shark were anything but beautiful bubbles. And my opinion had nothing to do with the sweat trickling coating my eyebrows. Only an idiot would have been clueless to how a kraken, crocodile, and shark were the opposite of beauty. Queen Bubbles also didn't hide her emotions well since anyone would have detected how the truth was in the subtext because of her irritated facial expression moments earlier.

I blew more bubbles, which consisted of a swan, lily, and a harp.

Wow. Maybe I was more cynical than I realized. I was better at blowing bubbles than I thought. It wasn't like bubble blowing was the type of game someone could pretend to be bad at.

Everyone clapped for me before Queen Bubbles gave the audience such an intense stare that her eyes should have popped out of their sockets. But no. They didn't.

Queen Bubbles blew more bubbles, only to have a knife, sword, and gun form, making her form fists before the audience clapped, anyway.

Enzo patted my back. "Good job, Alex. Maybe you'll win your freedom."

Two swans kneeled down on the ground by the pond in the distance and nibbled on something which wasn't visible from my angle. I closed my eyes while concentrating on blowing more beautiful bubbles.

Sure. A bubble's shape might have been random. But I could still be positive and hope for the best because I needed as many good vibes as I could get. A three-layer cake, dolphin, and a field of lilies formed, which made Queen Bubbles gasp. Although I hadn't apologized for

Queen Bubbles's latest spell of anger because losing at her favorite game was the least that she deserved as a result of treating people like dirt.

Queen Bubbles blew more bubbles, and three snakes formed. The audience didn't even clap this time, though, which was more than a little surprising. But maybe, just maybe, Queen Bubbles realized she would lose.

My latest round of bubble blowing made a dolphin, swan, and several roses appear.

Queen Bubbles's lips twisted. As if she ate something sour. "You must be cheating, child! I just know it."

"I've never blown bubbles before in my life," I said. "Perhaps you're having a bad day."

Queen Bubbles waved her stick at me. "Be careful, child! You're still on royal property!"

I snorted. "Yes, Your Majesty."

"I'm taking an extra turn." Queen Bubbles blew more bubbles, only to have three more snakes appear.

Resisting the urge to laugh was necessary no matter how much I wanted to curl up in a ball on the grass while my chuckling echoed throughout the property. But even I wasn't that dumb because I needed to win my freedom ASAP, and couldn't afford to take any risks. Although I couldn't lie to myself since seeing Queen Bubbles be flustered was more than a little amusing. She was the one who cheated by "inventing" a new rule and deserved her latest bubble blunder.

Queen Bubbles shook her head. "This mix must be bad. I'm sure of it."

Please. Queen Bubbles needed a serious reality check if she actually believed what she just said.

My latest bubbles were three dolphins and two swans.

Queen Bubbles crushed the bubble mix container so hard that it ripped before the remaining liquid oozed out of the bottle and onto the ground.

"We'll have to start over," Queen Bubbles said. "I can't help it that I got angry."

I wiggled a finger at Queen Bubbles. "You need to control your temper, your Majesty."

Queen Bubbles put her hands on her hips. "Thank you for your concern, but I'm not dumb enough to take advice from a child. Anyway, someone needs to fetch me another blasted bubble blowing mix container."

"Alex is now the winner by default," Pegasus interrupted.

Queen Bubbles rubbed her crown while rain drops crashed down from the sky, which consisted of even darker gray clouds now. "Excuse me?"

Pegasus snickered at Queen Bubbles. "You heard me, your Majesty. Crushing and disposing of the bubble mix counts as forfeiting."

"I doubt that," Queen Bubbles said, raising an eyebrow.

"It's actually in the fine print of Kangaroo Court code. It's law 444," Pegasus said.

Queen Bubbles clenched her jaw. "Very well. I might be a lot of things. But I'm a woman of my word. Your beheading is commuted, Alex."

I bowed before the queen. "Thank you, Your Majesty."

Showing her one moment of respect was necessary, regardless of how she needed to deal with her temper ASAP. She was still the same person who could go on a vengeful rant at a moment's notice.

"I can't believe it. You're free." Enzo opened his arms, inviting me in for a quick hug.

I humored Enzo and clapped his back. Then, we pulled back after a beat. We might have only been twelve years old. But we had admitted caring about each other as more than friends-even if we weren't sure what that meant. Although I couldn't even remember the last time we discussed "things" because everything got sidetracked.

Life was once again a series of adventures, since the future remained uncertain. Enzo and I still had to deal with the possible return of Ramona someday, in addition to how we were kind of homeless.

The rain hammered against the ground while Queen Bubbles forced a smile. "I've come to a decision. I'm canceling my tea party in favor of an apology party."

"What?" I asked.

Yup. I had every right in the world to have my eyes remain widened. Her comment proved she was unstable. Only a nonsensical person would go from wanting my head to be chopped off to throwing a party at a moment's notice.

Queen Bubbles rubbed her hands together while squealing. "I'm serious. There's nothing more that I like than an epic apology."

My lips quivered. "That's very generous of you, Your Majesty."

Queen Bubbles waved her hand through the air. "Nonsense. It's no trouble at all. I'm the Queen, and could do whatever I please."

Yeah. Her point might have been true. But there was no need for her to state the obvious. Anyone could tell how Queen Bubbles indulged her whims, since her random outbursts of anger were proof.

A figure stood out in the distance at the edge of the woods, making my heart flutter even faster. And I could have sworn the woman was Ramona. Although she was gone after I stopped blinking.

Wait. I needed a minute to pause, regardless of whether I saw Ramona. Sure. A party might have been great in light of my recent stress. But I couldn't ignore my stepmother problem no matter how much I wished I could do.

"Is it okay if I do something before the party?" I asked.

Enzo's gaze narrowed. "What are you getting at, Alex?"

"I want to go back to Whimsy and destroy my rubies," I said.

Enzo's jaw lowered. "Oh."

Yup. I hadn't misspoken. Getting rid of the rubies was in my best interest even if some people might have thought the idea was dumb.

Queen Bubbles crossed her arms. "Will it take long?"

"Nope. This errand is just something I have to do. But don't get me wrong. I still want to go to the party," I said.

Queen Bubbles sighed. "Okay. Fine. I suppose it wouldn't hurt to have a little time to plan the party."

"What about Marino the Great?" Enzo asked.

Sure. Enzo had a point. But I refused to be a coward because it didn't matter how much time passed. I would never behave like Ramona. Not ever. I couldn't. Although I didn't expect a medal for being selfless and destroying my fortune. I just had to do what needed to be done.

"It's a risk I have to take. But do you have anything that could get us back to Whimsy quickly?" I asked.

Queen Bubbles beamed her eyes. "Yes, I do."

"Could I please borrow it?" I asked.

"Of course." Queen Bubbles pulled something out from her pocket and handed it to me.

"How does this work?" I asked.

"You need to hold it while imagining the place you want to poof to," Queen Bubbles said. "Anyway, will two hours be enough time?"

I nodded. "Sure."

"I'm coming with you," Enzo added.

I chuckled. "I figured as much."

Queen Bubbles jabbed her finger through the air. "What are you waiting for? Get going because I don't want anything to interrupt my party."

Figures. Queen Bubbles just had to act intensely right, as it seemed like things were going well.

Whatever. Changing Queen Bubbles by convincing her to be calmer was a waste of time. I knew a lost cause when I saw one. And I therefore had better things to do with my time. Especially when I was in Whimsy. There was just no talking any sense into some people.

27

DESTROYING THE RUBBIES

Enzo and I stood on the sidewalk in front of my village's bank back in Whimsy. Yup. I used the word "village" because Flimsy's population only consisted of around nine thousand people and encompassed eight villages.

But enough factoids. I just had to admire the current weather. There wasn't even one cloud in the sky. Although thinking about the weather could wait. Sure. The streaks of sunlight beaming from the sky were nice. But choosing my next words carefully was necessary. Starting an argument with Enzo was the last thing I wanted. He had been there every step of the way, and getting into a fight would have been awful.

I exhaled a breath. "Please don't argue with me because I've made up my mind."

Enzo raised his palms. "Fine. Have it your way."

I trekked towards the bank's door without asking a minute to admire the big blue block letters on the glass door. Yup. Getting rid of my rubies was that important.

"How will you destroy the rubies?" Enzo asked as we marched through the cubicle section of the bank before going to the teller counter.

Please. Enzo shouldn't have second guessed me. I was a lot of things, but I wasn't stupid. I understood the value of having a good plan. And that meant knowing how to get rid of the rubies. Although I wouldn't blab my plan. Having a twinge of paranoia was justified. I could never be sure when I would see Ramona or Marino the Great. Yet I doubted that the bank was the best place to attack me. There were too many witnesses, which would complicate Ramona's or Marino the Great's vengeance.

"How can I help you?" asked one of the bank tellers.

We were by the first teller window, since the other three were occupied.

"I want to go to my father's vault and access my rubies," I said without flinching, wincing, or sneezing.

Yeah. Even I had brief moments of confidence.

She pushed her glasses up her nose. "Do you have ID?"

"No, but I've been here numerous times before," I said. "I'm sure you've must have seen me with my father."

"I need to see an ID." The lady straightened her long-sleeved button-downed uniform, which was wrinkled.

But I didn't have time to think about how the lady's shirt was blue like the letters on the bank's glass door outside.

Enzo forced a grin. "Couldn't you make an exception? Alex needs the rubies for an emergency. You must have children and would want someone to show them compassion in a moment of a crisis."

Getting angry with Enzo for helping would've been silly. Learning to do things myself might have been important. But I also wasn't clueless. And that meant that accepting help was okay. The world was too complicated for me to solve all of my problems myself.

She squealed. "I'm in the mood to be generous, which means it's your lucky day. Besides, I've never liked rules."

Funny she should mention rules. I forgot we were in Flimsy since I had been so used to logical fallacies and non-sequiturs in Whimsy. I even missed Whimsy's nonsensical approach. But there was no need for nostalgia. I hadn't been gone that long, and would soon be back in Whimsy.

"I'm going to walk around...I'll meet you by the door." The lady grabbed a key and walked by the other tellers who were still helping the same people they were when I first walked in line.

Enzo and I walked a few feet to the right before stopping at the door. A key clinked in the lock, and the door swung up. The lady was in front of us.

She gesticulated at us. "Follow me."

Peppermint wafted through the air. Yet I ignored the urge to ramble about the scent because I was close to getting rid of the rubies.

Our feet squeaked against the tile floor as we walked a few more paces. She stopped at a door with the number 112 on it. And that was good. The hallway went on forever since there was no end in sight. An achy sensation also jolted through my body. And no. There was nothing wrong with being emotionally and physically exhausted after everything that happened. It wasn't like I wanted sympathy. However, I had been through a lot since Ramona tried poisoning me.

The door opened after the teller fidgeted with the key for another beat. "Take all the time you need, but lock the door on your way out."

I nodded. "Thank you."

"Anytime." The lady walked away, leaving Enzo and me alone.

The vault room was the size of my bedroom. Yet there was nothing interesting about the design. It just had a grey wall and floor tiles besides the crates filled with rubies. I even had reason to gasp. There must have been at least fifty crates filled with rubies.

"I'm not trying to be annoying, but Pegasus broke our wands," Enzo said.

Please. No offense to Enzo, but I was one step ahead of him.

"That's okay," I said. "Everything is fine."

Sure. There was no telling if psychic magic would work in Flimsy. But nobody said I couldn't try. It was only our wands that didn't work in Whimsy, as opposed to psychic magic not existing in Flimsy.

The image of an ember formed in my mind while I elevated my hands so my palms faced the crates. The ember multiplied into a bigger flame as my mind dwelled on me, sighing at how good it would feel to rid myself of the rubies. The flame then multiplied in my mind before turning into a sea of red, orange, and yellow. Fire then shot out of my hands before lunging towards the crates.

Okay. Confession time. Destroying the rubies was smart. But my heart still lurched. My plan to get rid of the rubies came to fruition since the psychic magic actually worked.

The flames continued swallowing all the crates while I made sure not to get emotional. I didn't want the crackling swaths of fire to get out of hand.

I pressed my hands together, and the fire disappeared, leaving only ashes behind. Holding my hand out made the window at the other end of the vault open. The ashes drifted out the window in one swift gust.

Jerking my hand closed the window.

Enzo smirked. "You did it."

"Yup. But let's leave before someone lectures us about what I did."

We exited the vault before I locked the door and retraced my steps with Enzo. I even laughed after making with eye contact with the teller who helped us. Yet I didn't dwell on my amusement as a result of who stood in front of us on the sidewalk after we exited the bank.

"Fancy seeing you here, Marino," I said.

"Same." Marino the Great gritted his teeth.

No offense to Marino, but I had to think about his appearance. And it had nothing to do with thinking he looked like death. Something creepy still existed about his stringy hair, since I wasn't impressed with it.

Enzo grabbed my hand. Wow. Another check in the win column since he felt the need to be protective.

"What do you want?" I spat.

Marino gave me a dirty look. "You lost sight of our deal, Alex."

"Are you gonna kill us?" I asked.

"Nope. You'll get what's coming to you."

I furrowed my eyebrows. "What have you done?"

"You'll find out soon enough." Marino snapped his fingers before disappearing into a funnel of fog.

Thinking about Marino the Great's threat meant wondering if he was in cahoots with Ramona and freed her. But nothing ruined the happiness radiating from my face right now. Not even the red balloon that a kid at the end of the block accidentally let go of. My rubies were finally gone; it was a fact.

Enzo shifted his weight. "Are you okay?"

"Yes."

"Okay. That's all that matters." Enzo gave me a quick peck on the lips.

I snorted. "What was that for?"

"I'm proud of you."

"For what?"

"Destroying your fortune. Your inheritance dwindled, and you aren't upset."

No. Enzo wasn't wrong. Sure. Father had also left me gold. But it was miniscule compared to the rubies that encompassed the majority of Father's assets. But enough financial talk. Boredom grew old quick.

"Ramona can't kill me if I don't have the rubies," I said.

Enzo's smile expanded. "True. But we should return to Whimsy before we anger Queen Bubbles by ruining another party."

Fair enough. We couldn't risk angering Queen Bubbles even if she forgave us. Emotions were unpredictable, and there was no telling when Queen Bubbles would have another fit of anger.

28

THE REVELATION

"I'm impressed Queen Bubbles put everything together so fast," I said to Enzo as we stood in one of the castle's grand rooms after one of the queen's servants fetched us sometime after our return from Flimsy.

Enzo nodded. "Me too."

Several tables stood at the other end of the room with copious amounts of food choices, in addition to numerous water pitchers. The witnesses and Kangaroo court audience members were here, too. Someone also sat on a chair plucking a harp, which was nice because that added atmosphere. Witnessing the music was great since Enzo and I missed it at the masked ball.

My jaw twitched. "I didn't think I'd survive."

Enzo smirked. "But you did. Anyway, we still have to figure out what we're going to do."

I drew in a breath. "I'm glad you brought that up. There's something I have to tell you, Enzo."

"Is something wrong?"

"I saw Ramona outside after I won the bubble blowing contest," I said.

"You can't be serious ... Hanna dealt with her," Enzo said.

My stomach cartwheeled. "I'm serious, Enzo. It was only a second, but I know who I saw."

Enzo raised his palm at me. "Relax. I believe you. Although there's no reason to panic. At least not yet. I doubt your stepmother would kidnap you from this party."

"You're probably right."

Queen Bubbles put an arm around each of our shoulders. "What are you two rascals doing? Don't you know it's polite to socialize at a party?"

Enzo's cheeks turned white. "We didn't mean any offense, Your Majesty."

Queen Bubbles giggled. "You can once again call me Bubbles. Anyway, I was only joking because it's your party and can do whatever you want. Within reason, that is. Although that's just a matter of semantics."

I bit my lip a little too hard since an iron taste stung my mouth. "Can I have a couple more moments of your time?"

"Of course. Is everything okay?" Queen Bubbles asked.

"I wasn't myself when I insulted you," I said.

Queen Bubbles winked. "Did you sneak some blue fizz? It's okay if you did. I won't tell anyone."

"It has nothing to do with blue fizz," I said. "The magician I made a deal with helping me defeat my stepmother put some curse on me to be rude since I backed out from the deal."

Queen Bubbles stroked her chin. "Thanks for being honest with me. I guess I misjudged the situation. Although no harm done since we're friends now."

"Fair enough," I said.

"Believe me," Queen Bubbles said. "I know what it's like to have a complicated life. I had to banish my own sister because of being afraid of her scheming and greed. She even bullied my father so intensely that he got ill and died."

Wow. Another day, another fact. But I didn't have time to think about Queen Bubbles's complicated past. I already had enough to think about.

"Really?" I asked.

"Yup." Queen Bubbles rubbed her hands together. "But enough chatting. We'll have time for that later. You two should help yourself to the food first, since it's your party."

Enzo and I shuffled over to the food tables while chatter continued filling the room and Queen Bubbles scurried towards Killian the kangaroo and the monkey court stenographer. The scent of tomato and other herbs traveled to my nose, making me shift my head towards the pasta. I grabbed the serving spoon and scooped a more than generous serving of pasta because of my stomach's growling before getting my silverware and pouring myself a glass of water.

Okay. Confession time. I didn't just grab pasta and water since I also got a chocolate chip cookie. Although one cookie was harmless.

Enzo helped himself to some beef dish in addition to grabbing water and a cupcake.

We trekked back towards the other end of the room while people started trekking to the food tables. Laughing was dangerous, though, even if Queen Bubbles running towards the food and pushing people out of her way would be the highlight of my day.

Francis halted when he spotted us. "I wanted to apologize, Alex. I never meant to betray you. Queen Bubbles made me participate in that farce of a trial."

Hahaha. Calling Kangaroo Court a farce wasn't the word I would have used, even though it was exactly what it was. Then again, I should have known what farce meant since I was the one who read a lot.

"Don't worry about it. What's done is done." I took a bite of the pasta before guzzling some water.

Francis sighed. "I know. But it wasn't right."

"Thank you," I said. "Not everyone would be big enough to apologize."

Francis rubbed his face with his non-hook hand. "Are you two going to stay in Whimsy?"

Funny Francis should ask that question because there were a lot of variables worth considering, even if Enzo and I would have to make up our minds. My memory wasn't that bad because I still hadn't forgotten about how I could have sworn I spotted Ramona earlier, even if I couldn't be 100 percent sure. Enzo and I would also have to consider whether Queen Bubbles's mood swings were worth enduring. There was a chance we would at least witness her getting mad at someone, even if Enzo and I weren't the targets.

"We haven't made up our minds," Enzo said.

"Well, I hope you do," Francis said. "Whimsy could use people like you. But I'm not stupid because I know you can't live your life for me."

My eyebrows arched. "Do you know why Queen Bubbles is so angry all the time?"

Francis shrugged. "No, but I wish I did. It's a great mystery because she used to be kind."

"Did something bad happen to her?" I asked.

Francis shook his head. "Nope."

I nibbled on my cookie while the mixture of the doughy, sweet, and chocolate flavors electrified my taste buds before I finished the treat faster than anticipated.

Queen Bubbles walked back towards us with two plates of food, which were stuffed to the max with pasta, chicken, and beef because one sneeze could have sent her meal flying. Although now wasn't the time to dwell on how she had a more than generous serving of food.

The monkey court stenographer walked over to us. "I'm Chip. And it's nice to meet you under less serious circumstances, Alex."

"Are you still going to track down the crystal in the Kuku mountains?" Queen Bubbles asked while she still had food in her mouth.

I exhaled a breath. "Probably not. Why do you ask? Do you want us to stick around or something?"

"I didn't have the heart to tell you this at first because I hate crushing dreams," Queen Bubbles said. "But the crystal you're looking for doesn't exist."

I blinked. "What did you just say?"

"I'm sorry, but I had Captain Rickshaw look for it himself," Queen Bubbles said.

Captain Rickshaw tilted his head towards Chip, Francis, Queen Bubbles, Enzo and me for a beat. "It's true because I'd never forget the pangs of sadness rolling through my body that day. It was as if my heart broke."

Being honest about emotions shouldn't have been a big deal. However, his bluntness was worth smirking about. And it wasn't even because he was a man and one might have expected more control. It was Captain Rickshaw's theatrical delivery that was worth laughing so hard since I almost cried.

"And mine too." Queen Bubbles stabbed a piece of her beef before breaking it off and munching on it.

The grey, mundane clouds separated outside, allowing a few rays of sunlight into the room. Having a little more sunlight wasn't something to jump for joy about because the room had a draft. Although that must have been because the window was open. But now still wasn't the time to be blunt because I couldn't afford another blunder-even if having an open window during the previous rain defied logic.

"Could you take my crown off, Chip?" Queen Bubbles asked. "I just want you to scratch my hair for a second."

Chip finished the banana before throwing the peel on the ground. "Wouldn't you rather keep it on? It's so elegant."

Queen Bubbles grunted. "This is no time to be bashful, Chip. Now please take this blasted crown off."

"Of course, Your Majesty." Chip removed Queen Bubbles's crown and scratched her head while she continued gorging on food.

Queen Bubbles's chest expanded and contracted several times. "It's as if I feel lighter."

"No problem, Your Majesty." Chip put the crown back on Queen Bubbles's head before red flashed across her face.

"Why did you take off my crown? Don't you know it's important for a queen to both act and dress the part?" Queen Bubbles dropped her food and it splattered onto the ground. "Look what you've done."

Chip looked down at the mess. "I'm sorry, Your Majesty. I was doing what you wanted me to."

"I never once gave you permission to take my crown." Queen Bubbles paused for a moment. "How stupid do you think I am?"

Answering the question would have been dumb. So maybe, just maybe, Chip wouldn't be foolish like when I insulted Queen Bubbles during that blasted breakfast.

"Smart move, Chip," Queen Bubbles said. "Because you might be one of my most loyal people in my inner circle, but I would have had to have your head if you answered the question."

"Could you please take off your crown one more time, Bubbles? I'd like to examine it?" I asked.

Yup. Even ramblers had moments of genius. I had a theory, and it was time to test it. Being wrong was the worst thing that could happen to me.

"Fine. But be careful. I wouldn't want you to break it." Queen Bubbles took off her crown and handed it to me.

"What are you getting at?" Enzo murmured.

"Give me a sec," I said.

My theory might have been bizarre. But it was still worth testing because I just couldn't help myself.

"How do you feel, Bubbles?" I asked.

Queen Bubbles's mouth gaped. "Like it's the best day of my life. In fact, I don't even think I could get angry if I tried. Not that I would want to become enraged. I wish I could be light as a feather all the time."

Light as a feather might have been a corny saying, but Queen Bubbles' remark proved my theory. Although it was still conjecture.

"How long have you had your crown?" I asked.

Queen Bubbles sighed. "About ten years. Why?"

I turned to Francis. "Is that when she started to act like this?"

Francis remained silent for a beat. "Yeah. I think so. What are you getting at?"

"I think it's cursed." I put the crown on the ground and raised my palms at it while the image of a fire became etched in my mind. Flames sprang out of my hands and shot towards the crown before swallowing it whole. A jerk of my hand then extinguished the crown.

"It can't be cursed...Chip gave it to me," Queen Bubbles said.

Chip coughed before speaking. "It actually is cursed, Your Majesty. It's meant to make you raving mad."

Queen Bubbles's jaw lowered. "What do you mean?"

"There's no point in keeping this secret," Chip revealed. "The plan has clearly failed because it's been ten years, as Francis so eloquently agreed. I'm a spy for your sister. I along with others, are moles having aligned ourselves with your sister because we were her friends first. The crown was supposed to make you do something and say something stupid, which would have led to war. Although we failed to account for your isolationist views."

Queen Bubbles wailed. "This can't be true!"

"It is. We were always her friend."

Wow. I couldn't believe it. Queen Bubbles actually revealed her vulnerable side since I never once thought she would cry after I met her.

Although I shouldn't have been completely surprised. Being a rambler meant realizing life was complicated and Queen Bubbles was more than an angry person. Besides,

I couldn't exactly fault her since I now knew being angry wasn't her fault.

Queen Bubbles crossed her arms. "You were one of my best friends."

Chip snorted. "Wow. I thought you were a lot of things, but I never thought you were stupid. I guess you aren't as good a judge of character as you thought."

"Guards!" Queen Bubbles exclaimed. "Seize Chip."

Chip scurried away before propelling himself through the air and going out the window. Queen Bubbles, Enzo, and I raced towards the window and looked outside, only to discover Chip was gone.

"Where's the bathroom, Bubbles?" I asked.

"At the end of the hallway on the left," Queen Bubbles said.

"I'll be back in a minute," I said to Enzo.

Enzo put his hands in his pockets. "Okay. No problem."

I darted out of the room, only to have my back hairs prick up once arriving in the hallway. A hand clapped my mouth before I could scream. My eyes then shut after I yawned several times while a coconut aroma filled the air, stinging my nostrils.

Ramona was here. I just knew it.

29

A FACE OFF WITH RAMONA

I opened my eyes sometime later. Stars sparkled above and the waxiness of the full moon sprinkled down, providing a balance to the black draped night sky.

Looking down at my lap revealed my hands were tied behind my back in addition to how my ankles were also tied together. But jerking my hands and ankles free wasted time because they didn't budge. Glancing at my ankles and hoping fire would melt the ropes even if I could have gotten burned was pointless. Sparks didn't form.

Someone cackled. "The ropes are magic proof, but nice try. Although I'm glad you're awake because the party can start now."

Taking in my surroundings made me realize I sat on a pile of leaves while trees surrounded us in every direction. Hmmm. Perhaps we were in the woods in back of the castle.

"How did you break free from the trap?" I asked.

"An anonymous figure rescued me. He said he was a friend of someone you knew."

Hmmm. Marino the Great might have been too sick to voyage through Whimsy. But I couldn't help but wonder if he sent someone to free Ramona since her phrasing was telling.

I gritted my teeth. "How did the person even know where you were?"

Ramona snorted. "I don't know. I didn't ask."

"Are you still gonna kill me?"

"Duh. I just have to figure out what I'm doing because I've been winging it after I used a locator spell to track you down."

I sobbed at her, even if showing weakness might have been a mistake. I just couldn't help myself. This was one of those times when intense emotions were warranted.

"Why are you doing this to me?" I demanded. "Are you really that greedy that you can't live without the darn rubies?"

Ramona snarled. "Yes."

An owl resting on a nearby tree hooted, while its yellow eyes glowed against the night sky. But I didn't even wince, despite never being a big fan of owls. I had bigger problems to deal with. Like how I was gonna live. I still refused to be the kid who died at twelve. I deserved a good life after everything I'd been through.

I snickered. "The joke is on you. I went back to Whimsy and destroyed the rubies."

Hubris wasn't the best thing in the world. But I deserved every ounce of amusement I now felt. Ramona had done so much to me, and a part of me enjoyed how she could no longer have the rubies. Besides, I never said I was perfect. And that meant sometimes sticking it to someone was okay. The important thing was I did the right thing most of the time. Not that I should have defended my character. I just couldn't help myself.

Ramona quirked an eyebrow. "What did you say?"

"I'm serious. The rubies are gone. But I'll take you to my father's bank vault if you don't believe me."

Wow. I might as well have told Ramona she only had one second left to live. Yup. Her scowl was that intense.

"That can't be true ... You must be wrong," Ramona said.

"You're the one who is wrong!" called out a voice.

Hanna shot an arrow at Ramona, and it hit her right shoulder before Ramona fell to the ground. Hanna's shoes crunched against the leaves while she shuffled towards me before undoing the ropes and offering her hand.

Hanna grinned. "Long time no see, Alex."

"What are you doing here?" I asked.

"I never left Whimsy," Hanna said. "I've been in hiding while using a tracking spell to keep on Ramona because I knew she wouldn't be trapped forever. And I couldn't help but be suspicious when the spell revealed she was at the castle before stalling in the woods."

Something clicked in my mind. The rings Enzo and I had were supposed to protect us from being tracked. Perhaps we had been lied to. It was the only logical explanation I could think of. People weren't always what they seemed. And perhaps the man from the shop was really a snake oil salesman. Because I'd be lying if I said I didn't feel conned.

I glanced down at Ramona. "Did the arrow kill her?"

"It just knocked her out."

"Thanks for helping me."

Hanna sighed. "It's the least I can do after my betrayal."

"The crystal doesn't exist. It's just a legend."

"That doesn't matter right now, because we should get going before Ramona wakes up. Enzo is in the castle's great hall."

Hmmm. Another aspect I forgot to mention when Queen Bubbles gave me a brief history of the castle. It wasn't like the great hall was important regardless of its title. Queen Bubbles seldom ate in that room since it was for special occasions.

I frowned at her. "And how could you possibly know that?"

"Yours and Ramona's hair wasn't the only one I clipped."

"When did you even have time to get a hair sample from Ramona?"

Hanna giggled. "It's a long story. But I thought it would be a good insurance policy because anyone that screws over a child can't be trusted."

"Fair enough."

"You really shouldn't have done that because now I'm going to get rid of you too, Hanna." Ramona folded her arms.

"Run, Alex!" Hanna grabbed my hand, and we trekked out of the woods.

Fleeing was the smart option because Hanna was out of arrows. Being inside the castle would also be good since we wouldn't have to deal with her alone. Besides, arrows were a temporary solution and we needed something more permanent.

My lungs continued to have to deal with the cold as I balanced breathing with the icy air and running. It also didn't help how Ramona's cackles radiated through the air while our footsteps ground against all the leaves.

We came to the clearing at the woods' entrance while Hanna continued holding my hand before she lunged into the air and started flying.

My hair became ruffled while more wind roared as we approached a castle window. All the empty tables made me recognize the room in a heartbeat because it had to have been the great hall since Enzo was there with Queen Bubbles, Captain Rickshaw, Francis, and Pegasus.

Ramona hissed. "How many times do you have to realize I'm invincible?"

Hanna and I whirled around.

Great. I had every reason for increased breathing because of Ramona now standing in the air right next to us. Although I shouldn't have been surprised by Ramona's reappearance. She was a lot of things. But she was resourceful as a result of her tenacity.

Hanna craned her head. "I'll deal with her."

"No ... We'll deal with her together," I said.

Not being a coward proved best. Letting Hanna deal with Ramona by herself was unfair. She risked her life by helping me, and I refused to abandon her now. Ramona also might have been too much for one person to handle. And I wasn't trying to be unfair by my comment. It was the truth. I knew I couldn't defeat Ramona by myself, which was why I reached out to Marino the Great. Ficklewamper. What a mistake that was. Whatever. The deal with Marino was in the past.

"And I'm going to deal with both of you." Ramona raised her palms before Hanna or I could speak. Ice shot towards me in a matter of seconds, pushing me through the castle window. It shattered into numerous shards.

Losing all my hope was foolish. Sure. I might have been lying on the floor. However, Hanna managed to blast Ramona all the way to the ground as I went through the window. Figures. Hubris would be her downfall because she was a villain.

"What's the meaning of this intrusion?" Queen Bubbles said.

"No need to be intense, Bubbles. Can't you see Alex is hurt?" Enzo asked before offering my hand.

"My apologies," Queen Bubbles said.

"It's okay. I'm the one who shattered the window," I said.

Footsteps echoed. They were Hanna's. But Enzo didn't look at her, which was understandable. Sure. Hanna might have saved my life. However, Enzo was probably still hurt by Hanna's actions.

Queen Bubbles crossed her arms. "You better have a good explanation."

I brushed the bits of glass off me with one flick of my shirt. "Trust me. I do."

Enzo's eyes lit up. "Why are you bleeding?"

"It's complicated," I said.

Enzo locked his arms together, pressing them against his chest. "I thought you were taking a nap?"

"Ramona kidnapped me," I said.

Enzo turned to Pegasus, Queen Bubbles, Captain Rickshaw, Francis. "Can one of you heal Alex?"

No. Enzo hadn't misspoken. Magic might not have saved someone from everything. But it could be used to heal injuries that weren't life threatening.

Francis nodded. "I'd be happy to."

Francis waved his hand over me. I then took my hands to my face and shirt, expecting to feel blood. But there wasn't any because he succeeded.

I shuffled towards the window.

"Where are you going?" Enzo asked.

"I need to see if Ramona is dead," I said.

Glancing outside the window just made me grunt.

The fall from the castle window was two-thousand feet. Yet I hadn't gotten the result I wanted regarding Ramona.

Enzo touched my shoulder, electrifying every cell in my body. Or perhaps I was being dramatic. My body couldn't help tingling because of Enzo. But maybe that was okay. Constantly, being nervous was no way to live. Yet emotions meant I was alive. And for that, I'd be thankful.

"Are you okay?" Enzo asked.

"Ramona's gone," I said.

30

UP IN FLAMES

R eflecting on Ramona's disappearance was necessary, no matter how obvious the idea sounded. She had been more than a nuisance to me. She wanted me dead. Yet she was once again gone and possibly dead. Although it wasn't like I wished her dead. Nope. I just wanted her gone from my life.

Enzo shifted his attention towards Hanna. "What are you doing here? Alex and I want nothing to do with you."

"I've been keeping an eye on you guys and Ramona." Hanna removed her arrowless bow and put it down on one of the tables.

I reached for Enzo's hand while making eye contact. "It's true. She saved my life."

Enzo shuffled over towards Hanna. He gave her a hug and sobbed into her chest.

His actions were more logical than they seemed because most people understood how important family was. I certainly did. I would have given anything to have Mother and Father still be alive.

But no. They weren't.

And I couldn't do anything to change Mother and Father being dead. Although maybe things would be okay in time. I might have been a lot of things, but being weak wasn't one of them. I somehow survived horrible situation after horrible situation. Okay. I might not have been the bravest person and could concede that point. However, I hadn't given up, which counted for something.

"Were you able to find Chip?" I asked Queen Bubbles.

Queen Bubbles shook her head. "Nope. He's gone, as are some others who vanished from the party all of the sudden."

My eyes lit up. "Like who?"

"Evelyn, Smith, and a few others in my royal circle are gone." Queen Bubbles twirled a strand of her hair.

"I can't believe this was years in the making," I said.

Something acrid wafted through the air. But it took a beat to realize what the smell was.

"Is something burning? I smell smoke," I said.

Queen Bubbles grunted. "Don't be crazy!"

Killian the kangaroo hopped through the great hall entrance while panting. "We have to get out of here because the whole castle is on fire."

Queen Bubbles huffed. "Good gracious."

"Let's go!" Captain Rickshaw screamed.

Enzo took my hand, and we jolted through the air and out the window before flying towards the woods. Killian, Hanna, Captain Rickshaw, Pegasus, Francis, and Queen Bubbles were right behind. The crackling flames also happened to be growing louder and louder.

Everyone spun around after arriving at the woods' entrance. I might not have been able to speak for everyone, but I couldn't believe the castle was on fire.

Yup. Plumes of smoke and fire engulfed just about the whole castle. Crows then zipped by in a matter of seconds, screeching.

Queen Bubbles clapped her hand over her cheek. "I can't believe it. Who would do such an awful thing?"

"Three guesses," I said.

Queen Bubbles gasped. "You don't really think it was Chip, Evelyn, Smith, and the several other members of the royal circle, do you?"

I shrugged. "It's just a guess. Although it would be a good way to weaken Whimsy if your sister wants to take back control."

The flames and clouds of smoke continued rising in the sky while the castle remained scorched.

"What are we going to do?" Captain Rickshaw asked.

"First thing is first. We have to get my son." Queen Bubbles grabbed something from her pocket and threw it on the ground. The ball transformed into a circular ship-like vessel and was about the size of four or five beds. Several buttons happened to be below the black steering wheel.

"Don't just stand there!" Queen Bubbles screamed. "Get in the vehicle."

Using a vehicle made sense even if I would never completely understand Whimsy. After all, Hanna, Enzo and I were foreigners and couldn't poof to places.

I stepped into the craft while Enzo held my hand. Hanna, Francis, Killian, Captain Rickshaw, and Queen Bubbles piled in after us. Queen Bubbles shoved her way to the front of the craft before pressing one of the red buttons below the steering wheel, making the clunky ignition roar.

"Hold on tight, because this will be a bumpy ride. But if it's a war my sister wants, then that's what she'll get." Queen Bubbles pulled a lever. The craft shot backwards before lunging forward so fast that everyone held onto the craft's leather padding so we wouldn't fly away.

Being surprised about continued drama would have once again been foolish.

Ramona might have been gone in addition to how her death was dubious—I hadn't seen a body. However, my current situation related to one of Father's cheesy expressions about how a window opens when a door is locked. In my case, the expression meant it was time for my next adventure. Yet there were legitimate reasons for my stomach's churning because there were too many problems. Just dealing with Ramona, Marino the Great, or Whimsy's possible impending civil war would have been enough. But all three problems coexisting made my head spin.

31

THE QUEEN'S SON

Killian, Queen Bubbles, Pegasus, Hanna, Captain Rickshaw, Francis, and Enzo and I just stepped out of the craft after coming to a clearing in another woodsy area sometime later. Although the weather was anything but nice. And no. I wasn't being critical. The temperature was so hot that I would have drowned in the heat if it were a liquid. A little sweat even stuck to my shirt. Having a lot of bugs buzzing around didn't help either. But enough thinking about weather and insects. Everyone else had started walking towards the two green tents a few feet in front of the craft, and I was now alone.

"Are you here, Rex?" Queen Bubbles asked. "It's your mother. We need to talk."

One of the tents zipped open, revealing a boy in a tee-shirt and pants. He had curly hair. He was also a few inches taller than us, which meant he was probably the same age as Hanna. They were about the same height, in addition to how his shoulders were broader than mine and Enzo's.

"What's going on, Mom?" Rex asked.

Interesting. I had been so busy judging Queen Bubbles for her temperament that I forgot she was a mom. Whatever. Governing wasn't mutually exclusive with not being a parent. Authority figures had lives outside of royalty.

Queen Bubbles sighed. "We have a big problem. The castle burned down, and my sister is behind it. Some of the people who we thought were our friends are really on her side."

Hmmm. Maybe I had more in common with Queen Bubbles than I realized. Yeah. The situations might have been different. But I experienced betrayal just like her. Nothing would make me forget about the bad things Ramona did to me.

"What are we gonna do?" Rex asked.

Queen Bubbles shrugged. "I have no idea."

Pegasus chirped. "Look at that. It's not everyday someone sees a clueless ruler."

"Quiet, Pegasus!" Queen Bubbles demanded.

Thank goodness for Pegasus.

Making Queen Bubbles mad wasn't smart. However, there was no denying how we benefited from some comic relief. Forgetting the image of the scorching castle was also something I wouldn't forget about anytime soon.

Queen Bubbles frowned. "Where's your tutor?"

"He went for a walk yesterday, and never came back," Rex said.

Queen Bubbles's face turned bright red. "You've been by yourself for an entire day?"

Rex averted his gaze. "Yes."

Appreciating the beauty of this small moment didn't make me cruel. It wasn't like I took pleasure in Rex's demises. It was just refreshing to witness something mundane like a parent scolding a child.

Queen Bubbles shrieked. "Never mind that. We need a plan."

"You're the one who is clueless, Bubbles," Pegasus chirped.

Francis gave Pegasus a dirty look. But I didn't need to be psychic to know what an uneasy stomach felt like. I had angered Queen Bubbles enough times to understand how intense she was.

"I'd ask for your opinion if I wanted it," Queen Bubbles said.

"Should we summon the military?" Captain Rickshaw asked.

Queen Bubbles grunted. "I don't want to alarm Whimsy citizens."

"We don't even know what your sister is plotting," Killian said.

"Forget that," Francis said. "We don't even have proof about her and our former friends being responsible for burning the castle."

He didn't say what I thought he did. Whimsy was the birthplace of logical fallacies, and making an assumption was easy. Unless making assumptions was the expected thing, which meant a Whimsy citizen would do the opposite.

Whatever. I didn't have time to think about logic and how that might have related to Whimsy. My head throbbed enough as it was. I could only handle so many events before my head imploded or exploded.

And no. I was being serious. Father once told me a story about one of his friend's heads exploding after being unable to solve a problem. Although that was all he said on the subject. I didn't have the heart to ask him if he witnessed it or what happened after that. I recoiled just at the thought of Father's friend being in a bunch of pieces and someone cleaning it up.

"I don't understand why your sister would bother you after all this time," Hanna said.

"Don't ask me," Queen Bubbles said. "I can't explain her because she's always been out to get me."

Enzo winked at me. "What are you thinking about?"

"Nothing," I said.

"I know you and how the look on your face means something," Enzo whispered, jabbing my shoulder.

I raised my hand. "I have an idea, Bubbles."

Sure. I might not have been in school. But manners were necessary with Queen Bubbles. The possibility of incurring more of her wrath lingered in the back of my mind.

Queen Bubbles beamed her eyes. "And what would that be, Alex?"

"Dealing with my stepmother taught me not to rush into things," I said. "We should rest and come up with a plan later."

"And where are we going to sleep?" Pegasus asked.

"We could camp," I said.

Queen Bubbles snorted. "Please. I'm the Queen of Whimsy, and can't be seen camping."

Wow. I was actually glad Queen Bubbles made a cavalier comment. Amusement was better than being afraid of her. Knowing we didn't have to rely only on Pegasus for humor was good. We all needed our sense of humor in light of the current chaos in Whimsy.

"Fine," I interrupted. "We could stay at an inn. I saw a sign a mile or two down the dirt road from the campground."

"But we don't have any money!" Pegasus screeched.

Ficklewamper. That blasted peacock had to be a pain. Although I needed to count to ten under my breath. Being hypocritical didn't interest me. I couldn't criticize Queen Bubbles for getting worked up and then do the same thing.

Queen Bubbles scowled at Pegasus. "We don't need money. I'm the Queen of Whimsy."

The woman had a point. Sure. Her comment was cavalier. But we needed every possible advantage.

"Maybe we shouldn't go to bed. Your sister might stage a coup, Bubbles," Killian said.

"Nonsense," Francis said. "Nothing will happen overnight."

Queen Bubbles nodded. "Agreed. Anyway, I've made up mind. We're going to get a room at the inn."

Relief flooded me. Queen Bubbles was right, and my reasoning wasn't because she was the Queen of Whimsy. A room at the inn would provide shelter. And that thought comforted me a lot. Shelter meant having brief protection from Ramona. There was no telling when she'd appear again.

32

TIME TO CATCH A BREATH

Queen Bubbles wasn't just nutty. She was also a great liar because she haggled the inn's owner into giving us a free room. Although I should have backed up and explained the dishonesty part. The inn keeper was more surprised by an impromptu visit from Queen Bubbles. Yet she assured him that everything was fine, and we were just taking a spontaneous trip. The inn keeper even mentioned the rumor about the castle burning down. But Queen Bubbles said there was a multiplier bee problem, and she had no choice in burning down the castle. Whether the inn keeper believed her was a different story. Even I couldn't deny noticing his furrowed eyebrows.

However, I was more concerned about myself and Enzo. We finally got a minute to talk. We happened to be seated on the ground in the front of the bed on the left side of the room. Killian, Pegasus, Captain Rickshaw, Francis, and Queen Bubbles sat at a table on the right side of the room near the deck door. And I also couldn't forget about Hanna and Rex. They were on the floor adjacent to the discussion table.

Enzo grinned. "It's so nice that we're getting a moment to talk."

"Agreed."

"I think my sister is smitten with Rex."

A quick glance revealed Enzo was right. Hanna was giggling at Rex's jokes. Almost like she wanted him to know that she thought he was funny. Whatever. Hanna and Rex weren't my problem. I had barely gotten any quality time with Enzo, and it would be over faster than I imagined.

Enzo picked at his nail. "Do you mind if I ask you a question?"

"Go ahead."

"Do you think Ramona is alive?"

Enzo's question was fair. Ramona still being alive had crossed my mind. And I needed an answer to that question sooner rather than later.

I sighed. "Yes. No body, no death."

Enzo snickered. "That's fair."

Phew. Enzo agreed with me, which was great. Doing so saved time. No offense to him, but I didn't have time to explain why being skeptical about Ramona's "death" was necessary.

"It's amazing we've survived everything," Enzo said.

"You don't think I'm crazy, do you?"

Yup. Worrying couldn't be helped. And my opinion had nothing to do with causing trouble. My heart was just always thumping, which meant being aware of a possible problem.

"Of course not. I just wanted to know your feelings," Enzo said.

"It's just so frustrating because we don't even know what Ramona is planning."

"Or if she's in cahoots with Marino the Great."

I snorted. "Please. I can't think about that man right now."

My comment was serious. Ramona and being on the run from Queen Bubbles's sister made life complicated enough. Yet I couldn't forget about Marino the Great. I backstabbed him, and I imagined that wasn't something he could forget. Unless his death curse affected his memory. But that wasn't my problem. I needed to concentrate on defeating Ramona and Queen Bubbles's traitors in her court.

Specs of moonlight trickled into the motel room since the deck curtains were pulled back. I almost shook my head. Being surprised couldn't be helped. I hadn't realized how late it was.

Enzo squeezed my hand. "I'm glad I came with you on this adventure."

I quirked my eyebrows. "Really?"

"Yes, I belong with you," Enzo said.

I looked up at him. "I feel the same way."

"But it would be nice to have a moment of reprieve from all of our drama."

"This moment right now counts."

Enzo nudged my shoulder. "You know what I mean."

Yeah, I knew what Enzo meant. He wasn't off with his comment. I also dreamed of a life without Ramona or problems. And it would have been nice if having a great life was tangible. Life would have been boring if there were no problems, though. Yet that might not have justified drama and danger.

Laughter echoed, and I cocked my head.

Wow. Hanna wasn't giggling. It was Francis. Although I had a good idea about what caused his laughter. I wasn't naïve despite my age. I noticed when Pegasus asked the innkeeper if he had a bottle of blue fizz lying around when we checked in. The inn keeper even obliged Pegasus' request by handing over a bottle of blue fizz that was free of charge.

Queen Bubbles banged her fist on the table. "I'm sorry, but this conversation is too much. My head hurts, and I'm going for a walk."

Someone entered the room, waking me up hours later.

Taking a guess meant it was sunrise. A mixture of the orange, purple, and yellow stained the morning sky.

I stretched while yawning. "What's going on, Rex?"

"Speak, or I'll scream ficklewamper 1,000 times," Pegasus said.

"It's my mother," Rex said, trying to catch his breath. "She never came back from her walk last night. The innkeeper also hasn't seen her."

I tilted my head—Rex was right. Queen Bubbles wasn't here.

"What are you saying?" Francis asked, who still happened to be seated at the table with Killian, Captain Rickshaw, and Pegasus, while Hanna sat next to the adjacent bed on the right side of the room.

Rex clenched a fist. "Don't you get it? Something happened to my mother."

33

UTTER CHAOS

M issing.

It was one simple word. Yet the connotation was deadly. We had another problem to deal with, whether we liked it or not. Although it wasn't like we were getting anywhere. Nope. Having a productive conversation was difficult as a result of everyone shouting and talking over each other about what the best thing to do about was.

Spitting fire from my hands might have been gutsy. But it was the only thing worth doing. It wasn't like I wanted to hurt anyone. I just needed to gain everyone's attention.

Pegasus chuckled. "You've become gutsy."

Enzo frowned. "Please tell me you haven't become a pyromaniac as a result of enjoying burning all your rubies."

"You burned your rubies?" Pegasus asked.

"Yes," I said without hesitating.

"Who does that?" Pegasus asked.

"I wasn't trying to frighten anyone. But we need to come up with a concrete plan." The fire balls vanished from my hands.

Rex scratched the side of his head. "Alex is right."

Being arrogant wasn't good. But I still enjoyed praise. Thinking life would always be doom and gloom would have been unfair. I enjoyed having a few happy moments.

Francis snorted. "Fine. What do you think we should do?"

I shrugged. "I don't know."

Yup. I had no issue being that guy. The guy who believed we needed to do something, but didn't have a plan. And no. My opinion didn't make me a hypocrite. I was being practical. I only said I wanted to stop the arguing. Not that I had some magical solution to rescue Queen Bubbles.

"Wow," Killian said. "You don't have a plan."

"I doubt Queen Bubbles enacted a secret mission without telling us," Captain Rickshaw said.

Rex folded his arms. "And why's that?"

"She would want to tell us," Captain Rickshaw replied. "She was also concerned about picking you up and making sure you were safe."

Hanna twirled a strand of her hair around her finger. "We can't just sit around and do nothing."

Taking a minute to pause would have entailed chastising Hanna about how playing with her hair defined simplicity. But no. Starting more trouble would make life more complicated; not less complicated.

"We should look for her," Rex said.

"With what?" I asked. "Your mother has the craft thing."

"Then we better start walking or flying," Rex said.

Francis scratched his chin. "We can't cause panic."

"I'm leaving," Rex said.

"We should check out first because that's proper protocol," Pegasus said.

Giving Rex a sympathetic glance might have happened in another situation. But not now. I could only speculate if Rex had a temper like his mother. Then again, the temper wasn't Queen Bubbles's fault. Only a fool would have thought she should have been blamed for not being in control of her emotions in light of her sister's sabotage. Although it would have been nice to meet her sister so I could put a face to the name. Check that. Meeting Queen Bubbles's sister wasn't ideal. Thinking about one villain was bad enough because I didn't want to burden my mind.

"Don't be afraid to break a rule." Rex exited the room, slamming the door shut behind him.

Another second, another reason to laugh. Pegasus once told me a story about someone who wished she snuck blue fizz into the party and uttered the same thing Rex just had. The lady was more than a little irritated that there wasn't blue fizz at the event, which caused her to go off on a ramble about being too afraid to take risks.

"Come back, Rex!" Hanna called out.

Hanna trailed Rex, then Enzo and I followed Hanna. Footsteps soon echoed behind me, which meant Killian, Pegasus, Francis, and Captain Rickshaw were behind us.

I turned the corner in the hallway in a beat, and almost got distracted by the various paintings and swords hanging on the polka dotted wallpaper. But no. Getting distracted for another moment would have meant bumping into Enzo and tripping down the stairs. And I didn't need that.

"Watch your step," Enzo said.

I stepped down the last step before following Enzo a few feet to the front door. Hanna and Rex were already standing on the grass adjacent to the front steps. Enzo and I then joined them, as did Killian, Pegasus, Francis, and Captain Rickshaw.

Fog crackled through the air before I caught my breath. But I shouldn't have been concerned about the fog. Nope. The woman standing before me pricked my back hairs.

"What are you doing here, Ramona?" I asked.

Ramona bit her lip. "Relax. I'm not mad you burnt the rubies, and I also don't want to kill you."

I blinked. "You don't?"

Ramona shook her head in a vigorous fashion. "I know Queen Bubbles is missing, and I'm here to help."

34

MAKING A DEAL WITH RAMONA

I crossed my arms. "How do you know that?"

Acting tough wasn't about putting on a farce, so I wouldn't seem weak since Enzo, Hanna, Rex, Francis, Captain Rickshaw, Pegasus, and Killian were with me. Ramona needed to know I wasn't afraid of her. Even if that meant pretending to be someone I wasn't. It wasn't like I wanted to commit some awful crime. I just couldn't show one ounce of weakness to Ramona. Not after everything she did to me. Sure. She did a lot of things. But she couldn't take my courage.

"Fine. You caught me," Ramona said. "I was spying on you guys and overheard Rex talking to the innkeeper."

Hanna gave Ramona a dirty look. "Give us one reason to trust you."

Ramona sucked in a breath. "I wanna make amends because I'm tired of fighting."

Hanna cocked her head at me. "This is probably a trap."

"She can hear you," Pegasus chirped.

Leave it to Pegasus for having a sense of humor. But I wouldn't get mad at him. At least not right now. I deserved a laugh after everything I had gone through. Even if it was at the expense of someone else. It wasn't like I wanted to bully someone. I just happened to have overheard a funny comment.

Enzo glared. "How can you even help us?"

"I used to live in Whimsy before I married Alex's father," Ramona said.

"I'm sure you only married Alex's father for his money," Hanna said.

I grunted. "What are you asking for?"

Yup. I was that guy. The guy who got to the point because he wasted time. The guy who was skeptical about letting his guard down. And the guy who would never get rid of my healthy dose of skepticism that followed me everywhere.

"Let me prove myself," Ramona said.

Hanna snorted. "How will you do that?"

"I have contacts here and can dig up info," Ramona said.

Hanna blew a lock of her hair out of the way. "You, of all people, would have shady business connections."

Ramona exhaled a breath. "I'll ignore the comment."

Please. As if Ramona should have pretended to be doing us a favor. One nice thing would erase her wickedness. Besides, ignoring a comment wasn't complicated. It wasn't like she rescued me from a burning building. And no. I had no issue with being extreme by mentioning a burning building. I needed an intense example to illustrate my point, even if my teachers in Flimsy would have told me to think about nicer things.

I raised an eyebrow. "You can't tell anyone Queen Bubbles is missing."

"I won't—I swear on my life," Ramona replied.

"How do we know you aren't in cahoots with Marino the Great?" Enzo asked.

Ramona snickered. "I'm not. I haven't had any connection with him since he sent someone to free me from the quicksand."

Interesting. Ramona confirmed something I wondered about.

Yeah. I might not have had any proof linking Marino the Great and Ramona. However, I trusted my intuition. At least most of the time. Marino the Great was the one who made that threat against me after I burned my rubies. Yet he was smart when accosting me. He channeled enough malice to scare me, but not enough to accuse him of wrongdoing.

"We have a deal. But you have till tomorrow morning," I said.

Hanna hissed. "You can't be serious, Alex."

"We need all the help we can get," I said.

Rex rolled his eyes. "I can wait one day. But I'm searching for my mother after that."

"I understand," I said.

Ramona beamed. "Shall we shake on the deal?"

"That's okay," I said.

"Where shall I meet you?" Ramona asked.

"Here. We'll be staying till tomorrow," I said.

"Fair enough," Ramona said.

Francis squinted at Ramona. "Have we met before?"

Ramona clutched her emerald pendant wrapped around her neck. "I don't think so."

Captain Rickshaw's eyes widened. "It's not just Francis. You feel so familiar."

Ramona giggled. "I have that face."

"You have a nice necklace," Pegasus said.

A smile tugged at Ramona's lips. "Thank you. It's helped me out in ways you can't even imagine."

Ramona clicked her fingers and disappeared into a funnel of fog. Her vanishing wasn't odd, though. Living in Whimsy before Flimsy meant she was a Whimsy citizen and could zap to places as opposed to me, Enzo, and Hanna.

Enzo tilted his head. "I hope you know what you're doing, Alex."

I looked around my surroundings. Any distraction I could get was necessary. Like admiring the inn's front porch and how the roof was in perfect condition in addition to the shudders. They didn't have any signs of erosion. The sky-blue paint on the inn's exterior was also nice. It made the inn appear welcoming, since sky-blue was a friendly color.

Yup. I associated color with feelings. The inn's small stature also made the property seem cozy. The house was only two stories tall. The rock wall on both the left and right side of the three stairs a few feet in front of us also created a pristine image. It wasn't every day that I saw a rock wall. But that was me. However, the inn's sign in front of the right-side rock wall put the final touch on the property's image. The sign was violet and the letters K-U-Z-U-I-N-N were in big gold letters. There also happened to be two posts going into the ground on both the right and left sides of the sign.

Enzo puts his hands on his hips. "Answer my question, Alex."

Ficklewamper. I needed to stop daydreaming ASAP. Although I was too hard on myself. Daydreaming made life fun, and I needed as many pleasures as I could find.

I didn't even blink. "I know what I'm doing."

My reaction was fair. Having Ramona do us one favor had nothing to do with trusting her or thinking she changed. I hadn't. She was a means to an end. I also felt obligated to find Queen Bubbles after the time I spent in Whimsy. And if that meant letting Ramona help, then I didn't have a choice. I also knew better than to think she was honorable. Besides, I hatched a plan. Although I wasn't ready to reveal it. Not to anyone. Not even Enzo. At least not yet. Nobody could know about my plan. It was simple math, really. Adding more variables to a situation made life more complicated.

And no. I didn't feel guilty for manipulating Ramona. It wasn't like I went around using people. Associating with Ramona was just as necessary. For the moment, at least.

35

A DANGEROUS ALLIANCE

A trumpet honked, waking me up the following morning. And I almost jumped to the ceiling. And no. Being startled didn't make me pathetic. It made me honest. Hearing a loud noise first thing in the morning wasn't normal.

I looked around the room. The trumpet wasn't from inside the room. Everyone else was asleep.

Oops. No time to dawdle. The trumpet honked again, and I opened the door.

Ramona stood before me with a wheeled tray of food and a newspaper.

Perfect. Seeing a monster was what I wanted first thing in the morning. In fact, I would have even said my life was complete now.

"What are you doing here?" I asked.

"You said I only had one day," Ramona said.

"You found her?" I asked.

Ramona's grin expanded, showcasing her well-aligned teeth. Almost as if they were too perfect. "Yup. But we should wake the others."

"Why do you have a cart of food?" I asked.

"I told the innkeeper I was going to talk to you guys anyway, and that I could deliver the food," Ramona said.

An itch shot up on the side of my neck, and I scratched it. "How thoughtful."

Ramona honked her trumpet again. Everyone was as startled as I was when I woke up. Yup. My response was honest since a few people whispered, "ficklewamper."

"What's going on?" Pegasus asked.

My eyes drifted to the folded newspaper on the wheeled food tray.

Being curious meant unfolding and looking at the headline. My jaw lowered. No. The headline was mistaken. It said Marino the Great was dead. Apparently, the curse spread faster than he realized.

Ramona snickered. "Yeah. You have a reason to smile, Alex. I saw the headline too."

Whatever. I didn't have time to complain about how guessing what was on my mind made her creepy.

Hanna stood. "Great! You're still stalking us, and broke into our room."

Rex's jaw twitched. "Did you find my mom?"

"Don't leave us hanging," Francis said.

"Yeah, some of us have important things to do that don't include associating with homicidal maniacs," Pegasus said.

Thank goodness for Pegasus. We needed the tension to be lowered, and I thus had no problem with being amused. Even if my teachers back in Flimsy would have thought Pegasus's comment was rude.

"Yes, I know where Queen Bubbles is," Ramona said. "She's being held in her sister's castle in the village of Fafa, beyond the Kuku mountains."

Yeah. Whimsy had villages just like Flimsy. Although there were 15 villages in Whimsy since it was a bigger country than Flimsy.

"You don't have to take my word for it. I have proof." Ramona handed me a manila folder, which I hadn't realized she was holding.

Examining the photos proved Ramona was right. Queen Bubbles was in all the photos, which seemed to be in a dungeon cell. Yet she still had a nice view. There was a window in all of the photos.

"She's right," I said.

"What should we do?" Francis asked.

Great question, Francis. You had the courage to say what was on your mind. Yet I wanted to pinch myself. I shouldn't have been making small talk with the woman who tried to kill me numerous times. But life was strange. And that meant dynamics changed whether or not I wanted them to.

"We're gonna rescue Queen Bubbles, and I'm helping," Ramona said.

I handed the photos to Enzo.

"No way," Hanna said. "We have no reason to trust you."

"You don't have to trust me. You just have to let me come with you," Ramona said.

Pegasus chirped. "You'll probably kill us in our sleep."

"Don't be so dramatic. Besides, it's eight against one," Ramona replied.

"She's coming with us," I said. "And that's that. Everyone be ready in one hour."

Sure. I wasn't the most confidant person. But someone had to take charge because we would have continued arguing if I didn't take a firm stance. Besides, I hadn't forgotten my plan. The one I still couldn't tell anyone. Not even Enzo.

36

A DANGEROUS GAME

"No offense, Alex, but I think you're making a big mistake," Enzo said.

We trekked through the woods now while our shoes crunched against the leaves. Ramona was twenty to thirty feet in front of us talking with Pegasus, Captain Rickshaw, Killian, and Francis, and Hanna and Rex were a few feet behind us.

"I know what I'm doing," I snapped.

Getting irritated couldn't be helped, even if I didn't want drama with Enzo. Being concerned was one thing. But it was another to doubt my actions. I didn't need someone to second guess me. Although I should have been flattered that Enzo was concerned about me. Then again, his behavior was natural. Even if I wanted to chew on the inside of my lip. Enzo and I were more than friends, and his concern was expected to be more than he would show towards just a friend. Yet I didn't want any variables to interrupt my plan.

Enzo sighed. "I deserve to know the truth."

Fine. Maybe telling Enzo was okay. It wasn't like he would blab my plan to Ramona. That was if my idea could even be considered a plan.

"Pegasus is right," Enzo mumbled. "She could kill us. She's probably still furious you burned the rubies."

"You're right," I whispered. "And that's why I'm playing along with her. It's not like my opinion of her changed."

"Really?" Enzo fanned himself with his tee-shirt.

Yup. He wasn't foolish for being hot. More beads of sweat than I cared to imagine clung to my forehead. Bugs were also flying everywhere, which was more than enough reason to flinch.

I nodded. "Yes."

"I'm sorry I doubted you."

"Don't worry about it."

"I should have known better."

Accepting Enzo's apology was smart. Verbally beating him up over his concerns would have been harsh. It would have also wasted time we didn't have since we had to keep pace with our goal to reach the castle in Fafa by dawn.

"What do you think her endgame is?" Enzo murmured.

"I don't know. But we're going to be one step ahead of her by letting her think she has the upper hand."

Yup. I went there. Assuming Ramona had good intentions was silly. Not after everything she did. But there was no reason to show my hand. Nope. Not when I wanted to win.

My foot snapped a twig and I tripped. But being clumsy wasn't my concern. A loud buzzing noise was in front of my head. Enzo even halted. Doing so was logical and didn't make him a coward. Multiplier bees had just flown out of the beehive near my head.

Ficklewamper. Ficklewamper. Ficklewamper.

Ramona turned her head to stare at me.

"Don't worry, Alex. You'll be fine." Ramona raised her palms. Ice spat out of them before racing towards the multiplier bees, freezing them.

Ramona offered her hand, and I took it.

I feigned a grin. "Thanks, Ramona."

Ramona smiled. "No problem. I meant what I said because I have your back."

Hanna and Rex had now caught up with us. But their pace shouldn't have concerned me. Hanna still had a scowl present on her face.

"I still don't trust you," Hanna said.

Yeah. Ramona did something nice. But I still didn't trust her either. The only problem was Hanna had more guts than me. Playing nice with my stepmother meant believing her brief rescue proved she was a good person. And that entailed not giving Ramona any flack, no matter how badly I wanted to.

37

CLOSER AND CLOSER

Swaths of orange glowed in the otherwise blue colored sky half a day later after we finished trekking through more woods and came to the clearing.

Perfect. We achieved our goal of arriving at the castle in Fafa by sunrise. Although our journey wasn't without tears and grunting.

Hanna got the brilliant idea of flying when we arrived at the Kuku mountains. Going through all the mountains would have been a pain. Yet flying still wasn't my favorite thing to do. I couldn't help worrying about how Whimsy was unpredictable. And that meant considering the possibility of magic no longer working. Although that was probably a silly idea. Magic seemed to be everywhere in Whimsy. It just took different forms. But it wasn't like we could go through a randomly appearing door for our journey to the castle. There was no telling where each door went to, and we couldn't delay our journey. We also couldn't take the hover device and travel like we had when picking up Rex. Queen Bubbles had the device; not us.

None of the miniscule details mattered, though, because the castle really lurched in the distance. And we now just had to cross the bridge. The castle was on the other side of the pond.

Rex screamed. "Let's move it! We don't have all day!"

I snickered. Something funny existed about what Rex said, even though I shouldn't have laughed. At least during serious situations. Rex was right, despite sounding impatient. Rescuing Queen Bubbles meant there was one less problem to deal with.

"Rex is right," Hanna said.

Rex and Hanna led the way to the bridge as Ramona, Pegasus, Killian, Francis, Captain Rickshaw, and Enzo and I scudded after them.

I was also proud of myself while crossing the bridge. My heart didn't even beat faster despite the bridge's creaking with all the footsteps.

Yup. I had to go through the worst-case scenario for a split-second. But it was only for a second. There was no way the bridge would break and we would fall and drown in the pond. And I was right because we were now all on the other side of the bridge.

"Were you nervous, Alex?" Enzo asked.

Wow. Enzo knew me well.

Hanna ran her fingers through her hair. "I still think this could be a trap."

Creepy. Hanna stole the words right out of my mouth since I just had that same thought moments earlier. But I couldn't sue her for having the same thought as me. Kidding. I had no desire to sue Hanna. She was Enzo's sister, and I would have to accept her if I wanted things to be good with Enzo.

"We don't have a choice," Rex said.

"There's a chance we could run into Evelyn, Chip, and Smith might be here ready to attack," Francis said.

Rex glared at Francis. "That's a risk we're going to have to take."

Francis huffed. "I know."

"We should split up into groups," Ramona said.

Hanna's eyes lit up. "Great idea, Ramona. Rex, you, and I will be in one group while Francis, Pegasus, Captain Rickshaw, and Killian will have their own group and Enzo and Alex can be by themselves."

Ramona's jaw twitched. "I wanted to search by myself."

Hanna whipped her head back and forth. "You're silly to think I trust you."

Ramona grimaced. "Have it your way."

I might not have known Hanna well. But I couldn't say she was stupid. I didn't need to emphasize how I agreed with being cautious around Ramona. Check that. I didn't think we needed to be careful. We needed to act like our lives were at stake. Ramona had tried to kill me several times before, and it wasn't unrealistic to think she would try again.

38

A SHOCKING DISCOVERY

"We should go into another room; Queen Bubbles isn't in here," Enzo said as we entered a study.

Thinking this room was a study wasn't odd. There was only a desk with a lamp on it and a chair at the other end of the room by the window. A bookcase also hugged the wall across from the desk.

The book case wasn't squeal worthy, though. And I wasn't being harsh. The bookcase was almost buried in dust. Yeah. So much dust clung to the bookcase.

"It doesn't matter," I said, walking further into the room. "We aren't just here to get Queen Bubbles. We still don't know anything about Queen Bubbles's sister or what Ramona is up to."

Enzo nodded. "Oh. You wanna find a clue?"

"Exactly." My gaze shifted to the bookcase.

My jaw lowered. There were only a couple of books and a photograph despite how the bookshelf had five rows.

I squinted, trying to see who was in the photograph. Doing so just strained my eyes, and I shuffled to the bookcase.

The photograph consisted of a man in the middle. Queen Bubbles was on the left while another woman was on the right. Wait. I knew who the woman was even though her hair was blonde.

"We have to get out of here, Enzo," I said.

Enzo lifted his gaze off the desk. "What'd you discover?"

"Come over here!"

Enzo approached me. His presence didn't return my breathing back to normal. Nothing would. Not after my discovery. The names: Princess Bubbles, King George, and Princess Ramona were etched on the brown frame in gold letters.

"I don't understand why your stepmother is in a photo with Queen Bubbles and her father," Enzo said.

Reflecting had to be done, even if it seemed redundant. Ramona was the one who complained about her sister taking everything from her the day she almost poisoned me. But that clue only hinted at greater malice. Queen Bubbles vented about being so afraid of her sister's greed and scheming that she banished her to this castle. Her sister made her father so scared that he got ill and died. Ramona also mentioned how she lived in Whimsy before Flimsy back at the inn. And I couldn't forget about how Francis and Captain Rickshaw thought Ramona looked familiar.

No. No. No. Another debacle occurred regardless of how careful I was. And I even wanted to stomp my feet. I knew Ramona was up to something when she showed up at the inn, but I didn't fight her. Nope. I was an idiot and tried beating Ramona at her own game. The only problem was I hadn't known what the game was, which made winning difficult.

"Ramona is Queen Bubbles's sister," I said.

"That can't be true."

The door opened. Ramona stood in front of us, smirking.

Ramona cackled. "But it is, and I'm so glad I ditched Hanna and my annoying nephew."

"Are you going to kill us?" I asked.

Ramona rolled her eyes. "What do you think?"

"You should answer his question," Enzo said.

"How kind of you to always defend him," Ramona said.

I folded my arms. "Don't you want the pleasure of savoring your con by goading?"

Using reverse psychology was necessary. Ramona was a lot of things. But I could use her evilness to my advantage. There was no way she would pass up the opportunity to revel in her exploits. Besides, every minute she talked was another Enzo and I didn't have to fight her.

"Sure," Ramona said. "I might as well explain things."

"Why did you go to Flimsy?" I asked.

"I wanted a new life," Ramona said.

Ramona coughed, clearing her throat. "I genuinely cared about him at first. But I was attracted to his money and rubies."

"How do you know Evelyn, Chip, Smith and any other traitors?" I asked.

Ramona snorted. "That's a dumb question. I was friends with them before my sister became queen."

"Being queen means that much to you?" I asked.

"I was supposed to be queen after father died, but he changed the law because he thought Bubbles had a better temperament," Ramona revealed.

I raised an eyebrow. "Did you want to kill your father when you bullied him into trying to change his mind?"

Ramona sneered. "No. But that blasted Bubbles didn't believe me."

"Are you still in cahoots with the traitors?" I demanded.

Ramona grinned. "Yes. But I didn't count on re-igniting things, since the cursed crown scheme didn't work. You were my priority, and they reached out to me after they were discovered you, just like they were instructed to do. I still happened to be in the woods. Kidnapping Bubbles ultimately became more important, so we stalked you guys."

"Sounds complicated," Enzo said.

My eyebrows shot up. "Did you and the traitors burn down the castle?"

Ramona cackled even louder this time. "What do you think?"

"Did you kill Queen Bubbles?" I asked.

Ramona remained silent for a beat. "No. But it's only because I haven't decided what to do with her."

"Why trick me and pretend to be on our side? Were you that desperate to brag?" I asked.

Ramona shook her head. "It wasn't about bragging. It was about luring you into a false sense of security. Having the element of surprise is also nice. We're in a more rural part of Whimsy since I didn't want to draw attention."

"How come Francis and Captain Rickshaw just thought you were familiar and didn't recognize you?" I asked. "It has to be more than your change of hair color. You're a full-grown adult."

Ramona pointed to her emerald pendant. "It's because of this beauty. It was spelled to make Whimsy people forget me."

"Yet the magic wasn't full proof," I said.

"No," Ramona said through gritted teeth. "Most magic is never 100 percent full proof. But my cover wasn't blown."

"Was the story you told me the day you tried to poison my tea true?" I asked.

Yup. I hadn't forgotten about her mother and how she worried about spilling tea when Ramona was a little girl.

"Yes," Ramona said. "Mother used to hate it when people brought tea wherever they wanted into the castle. We also had tea every day until she died."

Tuning out Ramona couldn't be helped, even if she was still talking.

Yes. Her rant was my fault. But the woman needed to catch a breath.

"...Although things were at least manageable until Mother died. She balanced Father, favoring Bubbles over me," Ramona continued. "But I know. You're just stalling, Alex."

"Are you still gonna kill us?" I asked.

"Yeah, I am," Ramona said. "But maybe I'll let you agonize longer. You know you're going to die, and there's nothing you can do about it."

"Not today." I held out my palms before she could respond. Ice shout out of them and stopped right as it approached Ramona. The ice expanded into a coffin-like shape before encasing itself around Ramona. The ice could have even fit a few more people inside it. Although that fact was a matter of semantics. Enzo and I needed to escape, and that was what we did since we started running.

39

A NEW CURSE

"I hope the others are outside," Enzo said before we exited the castle and stepped foot outside.

Smith, Evelyn, Chip, and a few people from Queen Bubbles's court I didn't recognize stood in front of Hanna, Rex, Pegasus, Captain Rickshaw, Queen Bubbles, Killian, and Francis. They were also blocking the bridge. But that was a minor detail. Smith, Evelyn, Chip, and the others had a fireball in front of their hands.

"We have a big problem, guys," I said.

Hanna shifted her gaze. "We're a little busy."

"Ramona is Queen Bubbles's sister," I blurted.

"What did you just say?" Queen Bubbles asked.

"I'm serious," I said. "She confessed everything."

Smith grunted at Evelyn, Chip, and the others. "Enough talking. Let's kill them."

High pitch cackles pierced the air. Ramona now stood in front of Enzo and me.

"That won't be necessary," Ramona said.

"But they got Bubbles," Chip said.

"I need to cast my curse first." Ramona shifted her weight. "Yup. That's right. The curse is even more important than killing you at the moment. And I won't even need my pendant once the curse has been cast."

I gave her a confused look. "What curse?"

"The one that will erase every shred of Bubbles as queen in addition to making everyone think I'm queen," Ramona revealed.

I pressed arms together. "How did you even concoct this curse?"

"It was a gift from your friend Marino the Great," Ramona said. "The only problem is it won't work on you, Hanna, or Enzo, because you were born in Flimsy."

Ramona removed a vial from her right pant pocket. The liquid's color was purple. But I should have focused on what she did next. Queen Bubbles tried flinging fire at Ramona even though it was too late. Ramona had already flung the liquid out of the vial before blowing a kiss and pushing it forward.

Queen Bubbles looked at me. "You, Enzo, and Hanna have to leave now. You're Whimsy's only hope."

Ficklewamper. Queen Bubbles' comment shouldn't have been funny. But it was. Her tone and inflection were so desperate that I almost laughed. It was the type of dramatic response a person couldn't make up.

"We can't leave you," I said.

"It doesn't matter now," Ramona said.

My stepmother was right in a twisted way. The purple mist had already passed by Rex, Queen Bubbles, Chip, Pegasus, Captain Rickshaw, Francis, Smith, and Killian, and was continuing to travel north. The purple mist had also expanded into the size of the former castle in the capital city. But I didn't need to think about the menacing mist now. Everyone but Ramona, Hanna, Enzo, and I gasped and grunted. Almost like they drank too much blue fizz and didn't know where they were.

"What's going on?" Pegasus asked.

"We have a problem, and I need you guys to do your queen a favor," Ramona said.

Hanna stepped in front of Enzo and me. Interesting. She might not have agreed with everything we did. Like with pretending to give Ramona a chance. Yet she felt the need to be protective.

"And what's that?" Rex asked.

Ramona pointed at Hanna, Enzo, and me. "Those three just tried to kill me."

Bubbles squealed. "What an outrage."

Pegasus was right, even though he was annoying. Whimsy always helped people, and right now was no exception. There was a door behind me, and Hanna, Enzo, and I needed to escape no matter where the door led to.

"Run!" I headed to the door, then opened it.

Hanna and Enzo turned their heads and ran after me before I jumped through the door. Enzo and Hanna then jumped through the door before she closed it behind us.

40

NOW WHAT?

The fire's crackling echoed hours later while Enzo and I sat on a log in front of the flames. The sky was pitch-black, yet the stars and waxy full moon provided the smallest bit of light. Sweat also dripped down on our faces. But now wasn't the time to complain about heat as a result of the damp chill in the air. We were in a clearing in some woodsy area. There were also two tents behind us. One for Enzo and me, and one for Hanna. Although Hanna had already gone to bed. Something about feeling stressed about how things never went her way with guys. And that meant my earlier observation was true. Hanna was sad about no longer being with Rex and getting the chance to know him.

Enzo glanced at me. "You can't be silent forever."

"I know."

"I hope you aren't still beating yourself up about everything."

"I can't help it."

"It's not your fault Ramona tricked us," Enzo said.

I pouted. "I shouldn't have given into hubris."

"We need to move forward."

I looked up at him. "How do you always know the right thing to say?"

"Because I know you," he said.

I snickered. "Good point. Although it seems like you're suffering from a little hubris, too."

He grinned. "Yeah. I probably am. "

"I imagine Ramona will come for us."

"That's tomorrow's problem."

My jaw twitched. "That's a good point. But knowing I need to relax and actually relaxing are two different things."

"I just can't believe Ramona found a curse that powerful."

"I believe it," I said.

He drew in a breath. "I never thought I'd be thankful for one of those random doors."

"Me neither."

He gave me a pleading look. "Please cheer up."

"I'm not trying to be a downer."

"I just don't like seeing you upset." Enzo sucked on his teeth. "You're a good person, and deserve to be happy."

"We have nothing." I rubbed my cheek, swatting a bug away. Life was far from perfect, but I'd be damned if I let an insect bite me. Something creepy just existed about insects. Perhaps it was their ability to fly that unnerved me.

Enzo frowned. "That's not true. We've got each other, and Hanna. Besides, we also have our memories."

"Maybe we should return to Flimsy," I said.

"That'd be risky. We would have to fly or go on foot since we don't have the traveling hover thing or the object that Queen Bubbles gave you that let us zap back to your bank. People would see us flying, walking, or traveling."

I stood. "You're right."

"I know it's hard, but have faith." Enzo patted my back. "We'll find a way to survive this somehow."

If I felt like being difficult, then I would've argued with Enzo. But no. I didn't have the energy for bickering. Being alive was miracle enough, because my pulse hadn't stopped hammering in my ears. And I hoped Enzo was correct. My current predicament went back to that idea about how false hope was better than no hope. I mean, if I believed everything would be okay, then maybe life would be okay.

About the Author

Chris Bedell is the author of over a dozen novels.

He also graduated with a BA in Creative Writing from Fairleigh Dickinson University in 2016.